DEAD HUNT

By Kenn Crawford

CRAWFORD HOUSE PUBLISHING

3-1344 Grand Lake Road
Grand Lake Road, Nova Scotia, Canada B1M 1A1
Website: kenncrawford.com

This is a work of fiction. Names, characters, events, and incidents are the products of the author's imagination. Any resemblance to actual persons, living or dead, or events, is purely coincidental. The opinions expressed are those of the characters and should not be confused with those of the author.

ISBN: 978-1-989911-06-8

Edited by Michael Upchurch and Claude Bouchard
Cover Design by Luke Romyn (www.lukeromyn.com)

Other Books by Kenn Crawford

FICTION

Code 900: A Derrick Stone Crime Story *(thriller)*

The Saga of Bayou Billy *(comedy)*

The Misadventures of Mallory Malo: A Ghost Story She's Dying To Tell You *(middle-grade)*

The Princess Knights *(a short read for young children)*

NONFICTION

The Covid Chronicles:
Personal Pandemic Stories from Around the World: 2020 *(non-fiction, memoirs, poems, stories)*

FILM MAKING BOOKS

The Indie Filmmaker's Shot List:
Create film and video shot lists. Keep them organized in one book *(200 pages - 8.5" x 11")*

The Indie Filmmaker's Storyboard Book:
Create storyboards for your indie film or video shoot. *(200 pages - 8.5" x 11")*

For more information, visit:
kenncrawford.com/books
kenncrawford.com/journals
kenncrawford.com/128page_coloringbook

To my children:

Tyler, Brittany, and Cathy

Table of Contents

Thank you to Claude Bouchard and Mike Upchurch who took on the daunting task of editing my manuscript and helping me fine-tune the story. Thank you also to Randall Carruthers and Lindsey Burns for reading my early drafts and offering great suggestions, and to Luke Romyn for the amazing cover.

A very special thank you to my grandfather, Bernie Crawford, who always encouraged me to read; his love of reading and writing inspired me to chase my own writing dreams.
Thank you Papa RIP

DEAD HUNT

SOME THINGS ARE BETTER LEFT DEAD

KENN CRAWFORD

Prologue

She hurt.

Her battered foot pleaded helplessly as she stumbled down the abandoned dirt road. A thick, humid mist hung in the still air. On one foot, she wore a white athletic sneaker; her other foot wore only a blood-soaked sock.

Exhausted legs carried her wounded feet across sharp rocks, almost dragging them. Every other step broke the deafening silence with a soft, squishing sound as her tender foot met the hard, unforgiving road. The rising sun glared its cruel intentions of another scorching hot day.

Her bleeding foot tarnished the road with each cruel step, leaving a Hansel and Gretel-like trail behind her. Her blank stare resembled something between an unknowing daze and an all-knowing fear.

Remnants of the makeup that once highlighted her pretty face was now covered with dirt and dried blood. The tracks of yesterday's tears streaked her dirty cheek.

Her muscular thighs bounced gingerly with every step. Not Arnold Schwarzenegger-like freakishly big muscles, but a sensuous, feminine muscle that warned of powerful strength. She spent her high school years as a cheerleader, which meant she would put herself through daily rigorous training. In her freshman year at college she had been picked to be on the Cougars Cheerleading squad as a flyer, often called a top, because of her ability, dedication, and willingness to try the most difficult stunts. She placed her trust entirely in the hands of the bases, the girls on the bottom, who put her high in the air and caught her on the way down.

Cheerleading may have looked somewhat girly with scantily clad girls flying in the air to impress the crowds, but it was serious work - if the base screwed up, the flyer could be crippled for life, or worse.

Her Daisy Duke style cut-off shorts did little to protect her from last night's chilly air, or the harsh branches that slapped at her thighs as she fumbled through the dark forest, desperately trying to find the road she now traversed.

Her half-torn shirt hung lazily from one shoulder; her other shoulder was completely bare except for scratches, dirt and more dried blood. Her right hand held a death-grip on a giant, bloodstained machete.

She wasn't exactly the picture of innocence holding that giant, blood-soaked knife that she clenched so tightly it turned her knuckles white. She may have looked battered and beaten, but whatever had been on the receiving end of that knife was in worse shape.

Her toned waist, small stature and model-pretty looks hid the fact that she was a hell of a lot stronger than most people expected. But here, now, on this lonesome dirt road, the Cougar cheerleader did not have a whole lot to cheer about, and her strength was fading fast.

She raised an empty bottle to parched lips and drank imaginary water as the sun glistened mockingly off the plastic bottle. Her tired fingers released their grip; the bottle bounced on the road with a hollow thud then rolled quietly to a stop. An eerie silence followed.

She stopped her torturous walk and hesitantly turned to look at the road behind her. Fear sent a wash of tingles over her skin. She blinked slowly, as if saying a silent prayer, then raised her frightened eyes to the disquieting mountain road that was flanked by rows of spruce and tall pine trees. Everything was so perfectly still that it looked more like a photograph than the real thing.

Her small body shivered despite the rising heat; she knew what was coming. A faint groaning sound, barely louder than a whisper, chased away the silence. Her heart pounded in her ears as a figure slowly emerged over the horizon. Its unsteady gait resembled something between a drunk failing a sobriety test and a baby taking its first step. With the rising sun in her eyes, she couldn't make out any other details. She didn't have to; she already knew.

Another figure emerged, then another, until the entire width of the dirt road was an endless sea of staggering figures approaching at a slow but steady pace. Like an ominous shadow, they were always there.

She released a sound that was somewhere between a deep breath and a shallow sigh.

The mist had surrendered to the rising sun, the last of it trying to hide amongst the pine-scented trees, a losing battle. She did not know if she was walking in the right direction, if she was on the right road, or if she would get off this God-forsaken mountain alive. But she had to keep moving despite her exhaustion. She wanted to rest her aching muscles, her throbbing foot. Her exhausted legs begged her to rest, but she ignored them. She had to keep moving.

Willing her body forward, she gritted her teeth through parched lips and continued her agonizing walk.

The tiny freckles on her nose wrinkled as she squinted to focus on something as it glimmered in the blistering sun. It was a van. It was not moving, she wasn't that lucky, it was as motionless as the surrounding forest.

It sat halfway off the road, crunched into a massive tree. The van's windshield was shattered and bloodied. One of its tires was completely flat, void of air.

The scene painted an unmistakable picture. The tire blew, the van hit the tree, and the driver's head hit the windshield. There was no mistaking that.

A single tear ran down her pretty face.

She thought she had run out of tears but apparently, she had one left. She wiped it away with the back of her hand. Her socked foot screamed for mercy as she hastened her pace towards the motionless van.

She cautiously approached it, poised to swing her giant knife instantly and without hesitation. She witnessed what happened if you hesitated; to second guess yourself meant a certain and violent death. She had no intention of dying that way; she had no intention of hesitating.

With her knife at the ready, its sharp edge glimmering in the blistering sun, she wrapped her fingers around the handle of the sliding door, took a deep breath, then pulled.

A stabbing, metallic creak echoed in the stagnant forest.

The smell hit her instantly, rushing into her nostrils and down her throat. Her hand instinctively covered her nose and mouth as if that could stop the rotting odor of death from racing deep into the bowels of her stomach.

Flies buzzed around the driver's head; she barely managed to choke back a scream. She stared at the lifeless driver with remorse and stifled back the lump in her throat. Maggots crawled inside the driver's mouth. She gasped in horror. What little contents she had left in her stomach came rushing out. Puke spewed from between her fingers like an erupting volcano.

She escaped to the road and continued to empty her stomach.

Through watery eyes, she looked towards the approaching mob. Deciding they were still a safe distance away, she walked back to the stench-filled van.

Duffel bags were scattered, tossed about during the head-on collision with the giant tree. She quickly rummaged through the bags, half holding her breath trying not to vomit again. She found a bottle of water. Precious water.

She took a long drink. It was disgustingly warm, almost hot, but it quenched her agonizing thirst.

She poured some over her head as if trying to wash away the stench. It trickled down her face like tears, but she did not have time to cry. She wanted to, but she just didn't have time.

She took another drink of the warm water then rifled through the duffle bags, finding more of the sun-roasted water, a pair of running shoes, socks, and a t-shirt. She grabbed her cache then stepped outside to escape the stench that burned her nostrils.

Sitting on the ground, she grit her teeth in pain and peeled the blood-soaked sock from her battered foot.

She took a deep breath and poured water over her wounds. Without taking the time to let the pain subside, she used a sock as a makeshift bandage to wrap her blistered and beaten foot.

Pain raced through her foot and shot up her leg as she tied the shoe tight.

With a tired grunt, she lifted herself back to her feet, then quickly removed her torn shirt. With the mob barely more than fifty yards away, she stood before them naked from the waist up. She didn't have time for modesty; they were not interested in the view. They wanted her for another reason.

She dumped more water over her head and shoulders to cool herself from the scorching sun, then pulled on the clean, white shirt. It clung to her curves like a wet t-shirt contest.

She picked up her trusted machete and eased herself back to her feet. Her lightly-freckled nose crinkled as she gave the mob a defiant stare. Empty, emotionless eyes stared back at her. The emblem on the back of her shirt read: *"Cougars Cheerleading."*

She took one last look at the crumpled van that brought her here just two days ago and turned to face the approaching mob. Her lightly-freckled nose crinkled as she stared at them with pure hatred. Empty, emotionless eyes stared back at her. The corner of her lip curled in disgust as she turned her back to them and started to jog.

Pain shot through her foot with a jolt. Her thighs screamed for mercy. She had only taken a few steps before slowing to a fast walk. She knew she just needed to put some distance between her and them, and torturing herself further was pointless. She knew they couldn't move any faster; the problem was they never tired.

The image of the driver's shattered and maggot-infested face forced itself back into her thoughts. More tears raced down her face. She was tired, scared and alone. Alone, except for that goddamned mob. The disfigured, bloody, and relentless mob that just kept coming.

They only had one thought on their mind. Not a thought really, more like an instinct, because these people, if you could still call them that, had stopped thinking. Now they only had instinct. One instinct.

In the last couple of days she learned that whoever, or whatever they were, they were already dead. The other thing she knew about them scared her even more: They were dead, but they were hungry…

And the dead hunt.

Chapter 1 – Friends

The Cougars' cheerleading squad ran excitedly onto the gymnasium floor for their final routine. The Cougars had already taken home the gold at the regional and provincial competitions, but this last competition was the illustrious Cheer Expo, the big daddy of cheer competitions.

Tension and excitement filled the Halifax arena. When a few hundred high-spirited girls are thrown together into a competitive sport, things have a tendency to get a little nasty. Dirty looks were exchanged between some teams, while others were more vocal in their disapproval of their competitors. The sport may have been called cheerleading, but some of the girls were not exactly cheering each other on. There was plenty of nervous tension to go around as the undefeated Cougars took the floor for their final routine.

The Cougars' music blared from the massive DJ speakers as the girls performed stunt after stunt flawlessly. Double twisting with lots of high-flying aerial tosses to please the roaring crowd. The gym was alive with excitement and thunderous applause as the Cougars executed a superb routine.

The announcer read the judges' final decision and dubbed the Cougars the "Triple Threat." They had won all three major competitions.

Lucy and her two best friends, Lauren and Emma, anxiously packed their duffle bags as they talked about the grueling event and some of the rude comments the losing teams had made.

Lucy's perfectly proportioned figure often left men yearning in wanton desire and women thoroughly envious. Her silky brown hair framed her strikingly beautiful face, accentuating her deep green eyes and a breathtaking smile. Her soft, smooth skin tanned with just a hint of sun.

Lauren was a year older and a couple of inches taller than Lucy's five-foot frame. Both Lucy and Lauren were flyers and thoroughly dedicated to the sport of cheerleading.

Although Lauren often considered herself rather plain looking, her girl-next-door good looks made her anything but average. A smooth cape of midnight colored hair hung over her shoulders and down her slender waist. Her chocolate brown eyes sang of sweetness and seduction; a song that captivated the wants and desires of many college boys.

Emma was quite simply the lovable one. Where Lucy looked like a runway model and Lauren had the whole girl-next-door thing happening, Emma was delightfully adorable in her own perky, innocent, and naïve way. She was the same age and height as Lucy but slightly heavier due to her overly large breasts that looked entirely out of place on her petite frame. Her natural, wavy blonde hair and baby blue eyes made her an easy target for typical cliché comments: Blonde hair, blue eyes, big boobs and brainless.

Emma was naïve about a lot of things, but brainless she was not. She managed to keep an A-minus average with very little effort.

Typically, cheer teams had the larger girls on the bottom with the smaller, lighter girls on top, but Emma was unusually strong for someone her size, and that landed her a spot on the team as a base instead of a flyer. That and the fact that she did not particularly like being tossed high in the air because it scared her.

The three girls walked to the spot where Lucy's boyfriend, Paul Connors, said they had parked the van. Lucy was pleasantly surprised that Paul, Wade Adams, and Michael Blackwood had made the six-hour trip to watch the competition.

Paul, the local football hero, made no qualms about the fact that he did not think the girls were real athletes because he did not consider cheerleading to be a real sport. Whenever Paul made one of his "Cheerleading is not a real sport" comments, Lucy would tell him that athletes lifted weights, but cheerleaders lifted athletes. She enjoyed reminding him that football players could easily hold someone her size over their head with one hand, but so could little Emma. The difference was Emma had the strength and the balance to hold them up there a helluva lot longer.

"Cheerleading is about strength, balance and skill," Lucy often told him. "Football is nothing more than a bunch of smelly boys knocking the crap out of each other and patting their teammates on the butt."

That aspect of sports always amused Lucy; women were known to hug each other at the drop of a hat, while men always stayed a macho-safe distance away from each other. But when it came to sports, you rarely saw girls patting each other on the butt, yet in every male dominated sport the men did exactly that.

Cheer competitions bored Paul and he rarely attended them, so Lucy had been pleasantly surprised that they made the long drive to Cheer Expo. Of course, the boys had spent more time drooling over the other cheerleaders, but at least they had made the trip. Lucy, Emma and Lauren could have crammed themselves back into the smelly school bus with their teammates, but the opportunity to drive back with the boys was a welcome diversion.

Michael, or 'Mikey', as Paul often called him, secretly had a crush on Lucy. Everyone did for that matter, but Michael tried to hide his feelings, especially around her extremely jealous boyfriend, but sometimes Michael just could not take his eyes off her. When Lucy climbed into the van wearing a tiny pair of shorts that would make Daisy Duke envious, and a belly shirt that revealed just enough flesh to make you want to see more, it was one of those times when he could not help but steal a look or two.

Michael was a walking cliché of a stereotypical nerd. Back in high school he was President of the Science Club, the Computer Club, the Chess Club, and every other club where brain was preferable to brawn. His thick, Buddy Holly-like glasses were forever sliding down his nose, and he was always carrying a heavy stack of books that looked like they weighed more than he did.

Michael's feelings for Lucy were not what you would call a well-kept secret. Even Lucy knew he had a major crush on her since they were twelve. She didn't particularly like Michael, but she had to make sure that she didn't do or saying anything that he might take the wrong way and interpret as flirting, especially around Paul.

Michael had enough problems with Paul as it was. For the longest time those two hated each other. Not disapproved of or disliked; it had been pure, unbridled hatred. It was Wade Adams, the foreign exchange student from Australia, who eventually brought the three of them together during their senior year in high school.

Paul was, of course, one of the popular kids at school, especially around the hordes of girls who went all gaga over his muscular six-foot-seven frame. Paul wanted to be on the wrestling team, but there was no one big enough or brave enough to compete against him. The coach suggested he try football instead and that was where Paul made his mark. Of course, his mark usually came in the form of bruises, dislocated shoulders, and the occasional broken bone that he inflicted on the opposing team when he steam-rolled over them. More than once the local newspaper labeled him as two hundred and ten pounds of pure mean.

Paul also had a mean streak off the field. It was a cruel side of him Lucy did not like, but there was nothing she could do about it. The mean side of Paul came in the form of being a bully. If some unsuspecting kid rubbed him the wrong way for any reason, Paul made that kid's life a living hell, humiliating them every chance he got.

He did not pick on people for the sake of being a bully; in that regard, he was a bit different. "It's only people who deserve it," Paul would say, and as far as he was concerned, Michael deserved it.

The bullying rarely got physical because nobody had the balls to stand up to Paul, but it was not all that long ago when that changed.

Paul decided he wanted Michael's seat in the school cafeteria and told him to move. No one knows for sure if something just snapped in Michael's brain, if he was high on drugs, or if he simply decided life was just not worth living.

Michael stood up, as usual, but instead of picking up his food tray and moving to a different table, he looked up at the goliath and said the one word Paul was not accustomed to hearing from five foot seven, one hundred and thirty pound science geeks.

"No," Michael said defiantly.

"What did you say to me, you little piss ant?" Paul blinked in disbelief.

To his credit, or sheer stupidity, no one really knows for sure, Michael stood his ground.

"I was here first. You find somewhere else to sit." Michael said, his voice cracking slightly, but his resolve unwavering.

Walk into any high school cafeteria and the several dozen conversations happening at any particular time build to a numbing roar, but on this particular day, the instant silence that filled the cafeteria was far more numbing than the conversations could ever be. Jaws dropped in astonishment; anticipation hung thick as they waited for the beating that was soon to follow.

Not a fight; a fight would imply that the other person had a chance, maybe even a slim chance at best, but a chance just the same. The wide-eyed teenagers stared at the massive Paul and then at Michael. No, this would not be a fight. It was going to be a beating that Michael would not soon forget. If he lived to tell about it.

"Get the fuck out of my way!" Paul growled.

"No," Michael repeated, his determination resolute.

Paul's hand snapped forward and pushed Michael. To Paul, it was only a push, but to Michael, it was more like having a wrecking ball slam into your chest. The force of Paul's push sent Michael flying backwards. He was airborne for five or six feet before crashing hard onto the cafeteria floor and sliding a few feet more before skidding to a humiliating stop.

As the students roared in laughter, Wade got up to help Michael and quickly noticed that even with the wind thoroughly knocked out of him, Michael was still trying to get up.

"This kid must have a death wish," Wade thought.

To everyone who was watching, which just happened to be the entire school cafeteria, it looked as if the Australian was helping Michael up, but with the slightest of movements that only Michael could see, Wade shook his head *"No"*; his hand restraining Michael.

"You're outmatched, Mate," Wade said, barely louder than a whisper.

With a defeated look, Michael blinked knowingly, then Wade effortlessly pulled Michael to his feet. What happened next was even more unexpected than Michael's infantile attempt at defiance.

Wade faced the laughing football player, his Australian accent grabbing everyone's attention.

"Oy! I'm impressed. You knocked the little bloke down," Wade said as he walked towards Paul, fists clenched. Paul's laughing faded to a smile. "Why don't you try knocking me down?" Wade challenged.

Standing five foot eleven and sporting fourteen-inch biceps, Wade would not be considered a small guy, but even his muscular physique seemed dwarfed next to the bulk of Paul's massive frame. Paul laughed and snapped a right-hook so fast it caught Wade flush on the jaw, spinning him in a vicious circle.

Wade was no stranger to fighting and expected Paul to swing, but even he was caught off-guard at how fast the big guy was; people that big were rarely fast but Paul was, and his snapping punch left Wade bent at the waist and spitting blood.

What was more surprising to everyone in the cafeteria, Paul included, was that Wade did not go down. Sure, he was bent at the waist and he had to use one hand on a table to steady himself, but the son-of-a-bitch was still on his feet.

Paul stared in disbelief. Wade shook the last of the cobwebs from his head, stood up straight, and faced the big man.

"You hit like a Sheila," Wade smirked, wiping the blood from his lip.

Infuriated, Paul stepped forward and threw another vicious punch, but this time Wade was prepared for Paul's speed and sashayed away from the punch with the grace of a dancer, then crashed his own fist into the side of Paul's jaw.

Paul barely blinked.

He threw another punch at Wade, a straight left, and Wade ducked that punch equally as impressive. Wade threw another crushing blow to Paul's temple. He thought he saw Paul wince but could not be sure because Paul grabbed him in a crushing bear hug then slammed him hard on the cafeteria floor like a child discarding a broken toy.

It doesn't matter if it is a schoolyard fight or a bar fight, most people lack the skill of professional boxers and rarely stay on their feet for more than a few minutes; this fight was no different. Both boys rolled around the floor in something that looked more like a wrestling match than a fistfight as the cafeteria chanted, "Fight! Fight! Fight!"

The chanting brought the school principal, Mr. MacIntyre, and a few male teachers racing into the cafeteria to break up the fight.

"That's it, Connors," the principal barked at Paul, "you finally got yourself expelled! And you," he turned to face Wade, "you just might find yourself on the next flight back to Australia. Who started this?"

"I did," Michael volunteered.

The principal turned and stared at Michael in disbelief.

"Show's over." MacIntyre finally said, ordering the crowd of students back to their seats.

"Office!" MacIntyre ordered. The three boys turned silently and headed towards the principal's office with MacIntyre following close behind.

The cafeteria broke into a multitude of excited conversations as soon as the three teens and the principal exited the room. They were pretty sure the fight between Paul and Wade would resume after school, and what a fight that was going to be. They remembered the last time Paul was in a fight. Some big guy from a rival school had decided that Paul was not all that big and had challenged him to a fight. He quickly learned the hard way that Paul hit like a tank.

That fight lasted one punch, leaving the challenger unconscious and missing three teeth. But this Australian guy had not only taken Paul's punch, but he didn't even go down! Not to mention, he was fast and had gotten in more shots than Paul did! It was going to be one hell of a fight after school.

"Ok Michael, what happened?" The principal demanded as he closed the office door hard and plopped in the chair behind his desk.

Mr. MacIntyre knew his students, some better than others, but the students also knew him. If the principal used your first name in these types of situations, that meant he was mildly upset or maybe even a little pissed; if he used your last name, he was really irritated. But if he used your full name, you were pretty much toast. He usually called Paul by his last name.

"I punched Paul," Michael explained in a dead-pan voice as if the answer was obvious. "He only swung back in self-defense. I ducked and he hit Wade by mistake. Wade was only defending himself. It's not their fault, sir. It's mine. I started it."

Both teens looked at Michael with stunned looks on their faces.

"You...punched...Connors?" The principal asked in slow, steady syllables.

"Yes, sir," Michael said rubbing his hand, "it was like punching a tree."

Both Paul and Wade chuckled; the principal shot them a dirty look.

Mr. MacIntyre had a weird looking vein on his forehead that was just below his receding hairline. Whenever he got mad, the vein seemed to stick out just a little further and grow a little longer. Right now, it looked like the vein was throbbing.

The boys stopped laughing.

The principal looked from Michael to Paul then back again. He said nothing for what seemed like an eternity before turning to Wade.

"What do you have to say, Mr. Adams?" When he used 'mister' you could tell he was pissed, just not necessarily pissed at you.

"It's like my mate said, Mr. MacIntyre, self-defense and all that."

The principal was not buying it.

"Care to explain why you hit Connors?" He asked Michael.

"I don't like him."

Paul and Wade tried to hide a smile. It didn't work.

"Something funny, gentlemen?" MacIntyre asked.

"No, sir." They replied in unison.

"Listen, Michael," the principal instantly took on a more understanding tone, "just tell me what really happened and he is out of here. You do not have to be afraid of Connors."

Michael slowly leaned forward in his chair and looked directly into the principal's eyes.

"If I was afraid of him, I wouldn't have hit him."

Paul hid a laugh behind a cough; Wade turned his head to hide his smile.

Michael was making it damn near impossible for them not to burst out laughing. If that vein in MacIntyre's head throbbed any more, it might actually explode.

Michael could be a cocky son-of-a-bitch when he wanted to be, and it was obvious he was not the least bit intimidated by the principal's cold stare.

MacIntyre leaned back in his chair and stared at the three boys. He did not care how good a football player Connors was, he was a bully and he wanted him out of his school. He finally caught him red-handed physically bullying someone and could expel him, but Michael was making it difficult with his *they were only defending themselves* story.

MacIntyre didn't want to expel a top student like Michael because he finally had the courage to stand up to a bully, and there was no way he was going to send Wade back to Australia for defending himself. The problem was if he left those two off the hook, he had no choice but to give up his chance to expel Connors.

"Well, Connors," he finally announced, "looks like you got a *Get Out of Jail Free* card," he paused as he stared hard at Paul. "This time."

He stood up and looked down at Michael's deadpan expression. "I trust you've got that out of your system and are through punching students?"

"Yes, sir," Michael replied.

"The three of you report to detention, now!" MacIntyre ordered. "And Connors, I trust there will be no retribution on your part."

"Nope, I'm good," Paul answered with a smile.

Everyone doubted that answer.

"What about you?" The principal asked, looking at Wade.

"No worries, Mate."

"Good. If I hear that the three of you decided to resume your little shenanigans, you are all suspended. Do I make myself clear?"

They nodded.

"Don't think for a minute that you are fooling me with this ridiculous story," MacIntyre told them. "All three of you can consider yourselves on probation. If I even hear a whisper that the three of you were fighting, you are all expelled. Got it?"

All three nodded again as MacIntyre growled, "Now get out of here."

They left the office and one of the teachers who helped break up the fight escorted them to detention. When MacIntyre was sure they were out of earshot he let out the laugh he was suppressing.

"Michael punched Connors! I would have paid to see that!"

###

In detention all three boys sat, arms folded, without saying a word. Eventually, the teacher grew bored with the silence and stepped out of the room. They always did.

"Why?" Paul asked in a flat, monotone voice.

The other two looked at him.

"I can understand Outback Jack there picking up for you," Paul explained, "but why did you take all the heat?"

"You may not give a shit about getting expelled," Michael answered, "but there is a whole student body, and a football team, that does care. They want to win the championship this year and as much as I hate to admit it, they probably can't do it without you. I did it for them, not you. And I wasn't about to let this guy get deported for helping me."

Paul leaned back and said nothing. A few minutes later he mumbled, "I can respect that." Another long pause later he added, "Thanks."

"For what?" Michael asked.

Paul ignored him and turned his attention to Wade, "You're one tough, friggin' Aussie. That punch would have knocked out a lesser man."

"I saw bloody stars, Mate." Wade laughed. "That would have been bloody humiliating, to stand up to you and get knocked out with one punch. No worries about deporting me, I would have swum back to Australia in shame."

They all laughed.

Paul rubbed his jaw, "You gotta mighty mean hook yourself."

"I didn't think you even felt it," Wade said with a raised eyebrow.

"Oh, I felt it," Paul smiled.

"For the record," Wade told Michael, "hitting him is like punching a tree. What the hell do you have in your head?" he asked Paul.

"Just concrete and stuff," Paul chuckled.

They all laughed again; more awkward silence followed.

"Everyone probably thinks we are going to finish this after school," Paul finally said. Wade nodded in agreement.

"I think it's safe to say," Paul continued, rubbing his jaw, "if we go at it again, we'll both probably land in the hospital."

"Bloody oath, Mate."

"What?" Paul asked.

"True enough." Wade explained, "So… we good?"

Paul nodded, "We good."

And, from that point on, throughout the remainder of high school and into college, they stayed good friends. It wasn't every day that Paul met someone who not only stood up to him but would have actually given him a run for his money. He wasn't afraid of Wade, but he knew it would be one hell of a fight, and win, lose, or draw, he would have been hurting for many days. Wade was tough and stood up for someone, and Paul respected him for that.

He still disliked Michael, but he did respect the fact that even though Michael knew he didn't have a prayer against him, he still stood his ground. And more importantly, Michael could have easily had him expelled but had been willing to take the blame for the better of the entire school. He had to respect someone who put other people first. Michael still got on his nerves, especially when he caught him staring at his girlfriend, but he respected what Michael did and decided to leave him alone.

Wade and Michael also became good friends and invented him to attend Paul's football games with him. Eventually, Paul learned to tolerate Michael, and though he would never admit it, he occasionally enjoyed having Michael around. They still disliked each other for the most part, one good deed was not about to undo years of torment and hatred, but they could at least be civilized to each other.

Paul still made the occasional dig at him, but it was more in jest than to be mean. Paul learned that Michael was pretty quick with the comebacks and wasn't afraid to voice his opinion.

Paul jokingly challenged Michael to a game of 'knuckles', fully expecting Michael to be wincing like a little girl within a few minutes, but he quickly learned that Michael had more than just a quick mind; he also had reflexes like a cat, because it was Paul who was getting the sore hands from the game.

Even Wade tried, and Michael beat him at the game too. What Michael lacked in physical size he more than compensated for with quick wit and lightning-fast hands.

Paul and Wade started teaching Michael how to defend himself, not that Michael would ever need protection when he had those two around, but they both insisted he learn how to defend himself and start lifting something other than school books. It took some doing, but they finally managed to get his nose out of the books and into the gym.

"If he ever decides to put those fast hands of his in a pair of boxing gloves," Wade told Paul, "he'd be bloody dangerous."

"He already is dangerous," Paul answered on one of those rare moments he was actually being serious. "The rest of his body just doesn't know it yet."

Other than that one brief interlude of giving Michael a compliment, Paul constantly complained about Michael to Lucy. He told her that if Wade insisted on dragging that geek along, he at least had to try to make him less 'geeky'; he had his own reputation to protect. Lucy just laughed.

An outsider might have believed those two were actually becoming friends, but Lucy was not an outsider, and she fully expected that little house of cards to eventually come crashing down.

Lucy knew how much Michael irritated Paul, especially when Paul caught Michael staring at her. She didn't like the way he sometimes looked at her either, but she would be the least of Michael's worries.

Paul had a nasty jealous streak, and even Wade would not be able to stop him from stomping Michael into the ground if Michael did not learn to keep his eyes to himself.

Paul and Michael's friendship, for the lack of a better term, was putting extra pressure on her, and she did not like it one bit. She had to be constantly aware that she did not say anything to Michael that Paul might misinterpret.

It was all quite exhausting, and even though she was glad Michael was no longer subject to Paul's constant bullying, her life was a hell of a lot simpler when he was.

Chapter 2 – Road Trip

"Whose van?" Lucy asked as she threw her duffel bag into the blue Chevy.

"My sponsor family said I could borrow it so we could come support you. Team spirit and all," Wade smirked.

Lauren spoke up. "Team spirit hell, you came here to see tits and ass."

"Really? I didn't even notice," Wade's smile broadened. "There were Sheilas there?"

"You didn't notice?" Emma laughed. "Then why were you tripping over your own tongues? The three of you looked like a pack of dogs in heat."

They all laughed, then the three girls each gave Wade a warm 'Welcome Back' hug. When his time as an exchange student had ended and he to move back to Australia, Wade decided that each summer he would fly back to Canada to visit his friends. His sponsor family during his stay in high school were always excited to see him and were more than happy to give him a place to stay whenever he visited. They considered him part of their family, as did Wade.

"So, why are you driving?" Lucy asked Paul as he slid behind the wheel.

"Wade drove up, I'm driving back. Hey, Emma," Paul snickered, turning towards the back seats, "what does a blonde say after sex?"

"What?" Emma asked, never knowing what lame blonde joke Paul was going to come up with next.

"You guys all play on the same team?" Paul laughed.

All three girls groaned and rolled their eyes.

"Speaking of playing on the same team," Lauren announced excitedly, "did you hear the latest about that slut, Kelly Gets?"

"What's your beef with her anyway?" Emma asked. "And why does everyone call her Kelly Gets? Her name is Kelly Peterson!"

"Oh, my God, Emma, I can't believe you're that naive," Lauren answered.

"What?" Emma asked.

"Gets, as in every man 'gets' whatever he wants," Lucy explained.

"Really?" Emma's eyes opened wide in shocked disbelief.

"I heard she took on the whole football team," Lauren said with more than a hint of disgust in her voice. Lucy shot a dirty look at Paul.

"I never touched her," Paul said defensively. "I wouldn't fuck that skank with Mikey's dick."

"I wouldn't let you," Michael answered. Everyone laughed.

"Well, most of the team. Same diff," Lauren added.

"Why would she do that?" Emma asked. "It's not like she's ugly and couldn't get anyone to notice her."

"My dear, sweet little naive Emma," Lauren laughed, "it has nothing to do with getting men to notice her. Kelly Gets is a slut, plain and simple. And apparently, it takes a football team to satisfy her."

"Wow," Emma was confused, "if she's that easy, why would men even have anything to do with her? Aren't they worried about STDs?"

Lauren placed a hand on Emma's shoulder and explained, "Because men are pigs, sweetie. They can only think with one head at a time, and the little one is the one they usually think with. They will stick it in anything that opens their legs for them."

"Not everyone," Michael corrected her.

"Bullshit," Lauren argued. "You're all alike. You'd screw a hole in a tree stump if you needed to get your rocks off."

"Hey Lauren, you're in college now," Michael answered, "maybe you should quit it with the high school drama."

"Bite me," Lauren answered.

"Well that was mature," Michael responded.

"Listen you little creep---" Lauren started to say before Lucy cut her off.

"Enough!" Lucy cut her off. "The both of you grow up. Jeeze."

Wade popped in a CD and cranked the volume. The sounds of deep hip-hop bass lines rattled the van's tiny speakers, drowning out any possibility of further conversation.

Several hours later they were crossing the Canso Causeway from mainland Nova Scotia to Cape Breton Island. The Causeway was 4,500 feet long and the only road on and off the island.

The rest of the trip continued to be rather uneventful as song after song pounded the speakers. Paul tried a few more blonde jokes but couldn't get any more of a response than the girls rolling their eyes. Wade laughed at a few. Michael barely smiled.

The girls were exhausted from the competition and the long drive. Lauren and Emma couldn't keep their eyes open despite the loud music. The gang drove through the Whycocomaugh Reservation and then through the village of Baddeck.

"What the hell kinda language is that?" Wade asked, pointing at the huge sign as they approached the turn to St. Anne's.

"Gaelic," Emma answered.

"What does is it say?" he asked.

"One hundred thousand welcomes," she announced

"I can see that," Wade laughed as he pointed to the English version printed below the Gaelic one. "I meant how do you say it in Gaelic?"

"Caid Mille Failte," Emma explained without giving it a second thought.

"You're pretty smart for a dumb blonde," Wade laughed jokingly.

"Tapadh leat," she replied.

"Huh?" Wade asked.

"Thank you," she explained as she batted her pretty blue eyes.

"She's pretty damn cute too", Wade thought as he stared into her baby blue eyes a longer than he should have. He pulled his eyes away from her as they reached the base of Kelly's Mountain.

At the foot of the mountain was the turn off for the tiny village of Englishtown, home of Giant MacAskill. The three boys had stopped at the museum on the trip up to the competition to see how big this giant really was. They learned the Cape Breton Giant stood seven foot nine and weighed 425 pounds. His shoulders were measured at forty-four inches wide while his hands were eight inches wide and a foot long.

"This guy even makes you look small," Michael suggested as he snapped a picture of Paul standing next to the life-sized statue. Paul laughed, but when he saw the picture, he knew Michael was right; Giant MacAskill did make him look small.

The guys wanted to stop again on the way back to show the girls the museum, but a thick fog was rolling in, so they decided to just keep driving before it got worse. As they approached the top of Kelly's Mountain it got worse... much worse. Visibility was all but gone and the road seemed to literally disappear in front of their eyes.

Paul slowed the van down to a crawl, desperately trying to keep from driving over the side of the steep mountain. He'd heard rumors that the fog on Kelly's got as thick as pea soup, and he now knew exactly what those people had meant. He didn't even know he was driving off the road until the van scraped against a guard rail, scaring everyone in the van, including him.

"Drive in the middle of the road," Michael suggested.

"Why the hell would I do that?" Paul snapped back. "I could get creamed by a truck coming the other way, you idiot!"

"Because you're gonna drive off the mountain if you don't, moron!" Michael told him, "You can't see more than a foot in front of the van, so keep the yellow line between the headlights. That way it's impossible to go off the road."

"Great idea," Paul rolled his eyes. "And what happens if one of those big-ass trucks come?"

"You'll see their headlights. So, pull over to the middle of the road before you kill us!"

Paul knew it was a good idea. He just hated to admit somebody had a better idea than him, especially Michael.

Paul eased the van over until the yellow line was between his headlights and slowly crept over Kelly's Mountain. Much to their surprise and appreciation, not a single vehicle came the other way. As they reached the bottom of the mountain, they literally drove out of the fog as if they drove through a greyish white wall, but their relief was short lived. At the base of Kelly's Mountain red and blue flashing lights from a parked police car and a "Bridge Out" sign welcomed them.

Normally a 'bridge out' sign was no big deal, but Cape Breton, although known as an island, was actually comprised of two islands; the Atlantic Ocean ran through each end until they met in the middle at the Bras D'or Lakes, a freshwater lake famed for its sail boating and spectacular views. The combination of fresh and saltwater gave the Bras D'or Lakes a unique ecosystem. The Seal Island Bridge was the largest bridge on Cape Breton, and the only way to cross over at this end.

A thick, burly man got out of the police cruiser and eyed the van cautiously as it rolled to a stop. Paul rolled down the tinted window as the cop approached.

"You lost?" the cop asked.

Paul motioned his head to the bridge, "What's the problem?"

The cop looked at Paul for a few seconds before answering, but it was long enough for Paul to notice the cop looked like he was ready to snarl. The cop nodded towards the 'bridge out' sign.

"If you actually knew how to read, what do you think that big sign over there would say?"

"Jesus," Paul responded, "who pissed in your corn flakes?"

"Listen smart ass," the cop growled, "a car filled with partying teenagers tried passing an eighteen-wheeler and slammed head-on with an oncoming car. The tanker jackknifed and exploded, and a lot of innocent people were killed here, so I'm really not in the mood for your stupid questions because you're not smart enough to read the signs."

"Hard to see the signs when the fog is so thick we could barely see the road!" Paul snapped back.

"You're wearing my patience thin, boy," the cop sneered. "So I suggest you go back to wherever the hell it was you came from."

Paul, who had little respect for authority figures and even less respect for cops, wasn't smart enough to be intimidated or quiet.

"That's what I'm trying to do, get back to where we came from. Maybe you heard of it, it's called Glace Bay… and it's on that side of the bridge," Paul said sarcastically, pointing across the bridge.

"That's it!" The cop barked as he reached for the door handle.

Lucy quickly leaned over Paul towards the open window.

"Excuse me, sir," she flirted in her best sexy voice.

The cop was instantly pacified as his eyes traced the contours of her tight and revealing shirt before looking her in the eye. She had that effect on men, and she used it whenever it was to her advantage. She leaned out the window, crossing her arms so they squeezed her breasts together, enhancing her cleavage.

The cop's eyes instantly dropped again to take in the view.

"Bat your eyelashes, lick your lips, show a little cleavage, and you can have a man eating out of your hands in seconds," Lucy thought. It was so easy it was embarrassing.

"Is there another way over?" She asked in a sultry voice. "We really don't want to drive all the way back to the causeway and go through St. Peter's. I'm really tired and I just wanna go to bed."

The cop swallowed a lump in his throat and forced his eyes away from her cleavage. She licked her lips and smiled seductively.

"Men are pathetically predictable," she thought.

The cop, his chest now stuck out like an army drill sergeant, tried to compose himself.

"W-w-well," he cleared his throat and tried again. "When you get to Little Narrows, turn left. There's a cable ferry that can take you across the channel. It might still be operating. If not, then you have no choice but to take the long way around."

He looked at the other girls. "I suggest you girls phone your parents and let them know where you are," he looked a Paul, "and who you are with. They might want to rent a helicopter to come get you."

"What the hell is that supposed to mean?" Paul blurted.

"Shut up, Paul," Lucy hissed as she elbowed him.

"Yeah, Paul," the cop said matter-of-factly. "That's good advice. Nothing would give me greater pleasure than throwing your sarcastic ass in jail. But the jail is on that side of the bridge, and I don't feel like babysitting you all night. So turn this rig around and get going before I change my mind."

"Thank you, officer," Lucy winked as she crawled back into the van.

Paul dropped the van in reverse and eased it around. Without warning, he floored the accelerator, throwing everyone in the van backwards and spraying dirt at the cop.

"I hate that kid!" the cop grumbled as he brushed off his uniform.

"You're an asshole!" Lucy yelled as she picked herself up off the van floor and slapped the back of Paul's head.

"Oh, my god, you are such a flirt!" Lauren laughed at Lucy.

"It got us directions didn't it?" Lucy replied with a smile. "And it kept big mouth here out of jail. Paul, you really should learn when to shut the hell up."

"He started it!" Paul snapped.

"He started it!" Lucy repeated mockingly. "You can be such a child sometimes."

Lucy turned to take her seat and noticed Lauren had moved up and sat next to Emma. Lucy stared at the empty seat next to Michael. Lauren just smiled but Lucy shot her a dirty look as she took the seat next to Michael who smiled briefly but said nothing.

"Whatever you do," Lucy silently ordered Michael, *"don't stare at me, and please don't do something stupid like look down the front of my shirt or Paul will freak. I'm going to kill Lauren, she knows better."*

A few seconds later, as if Michael heard her silent plea, he turned his head away and stared out the window.

"Thank you," Lucy thought as she looked to the front of the van just in time for Paul to look in the rearview mirror. His eyes narrowed accusingly when he saw her sitting next to Michael, but as the van drove back into the wall of fog, his focus went back to the task at hand. They all stared silently ahead as if everyone's eyes were needed to navigate their way through the thick fog. With the yellow line between the headlights, the van crawled back up and over Kelly's Mountain.

"Why don't we just go to Margaree?" Lucy suggested when the van broke free of the terrifying fog.

"That's a great idea," Emma chimed in.

"My parents have a cabin in Margaree Valley." Lucy continued. "We could go there for the night instead of driving the long way around."

"A cabin in the woods with three girls. Works for me," Paul joked.

"And we can call our parents," Emma added, "in case they want to rent a helicopter."

The van filled with laughter.

"Hey, Emma," Paul smiled, "what do you get when a blonde dyes her hair brown?"

"I don't know," she answered.

"Artificial Intelligence!" Paul roared as Emma rolled her eyes.

"When you pass Baddeck," Lucy explained, ignoring Paul's lame joke, "turn right at the Red Barn. You can't miss it. Then just follow the signs."

As the trip wore on, one by one the tired passengers fell asleep. Lucy had to make sure she leaned far away from Michael. If she accidentally leaned on Michael, or he on her, Michael would probably not wake up because Paul might kill him while he slept.

"I don't know why he gets so jealous." Lucy thought, *"It's not like I ever gave him a reason to be jealous. It's Michael for crying out loud."*

Paul turned at the Red Barn Gift Shop and Restaurant and navigated the winding and steep roads of Hunter's Mountain.

Two hours later, the van jolted to a stop, startling everyone awake.

"Where are we?" Michael asked groggily.

"Beats the hell outta me," Paul answered.

"Huh?" Lucy mumbled as she wiped the sleep from her eyes.

"There's the ocean on our left so we must be getting close," Paul suggested.

"Ocean?" Lucy answered as she moved towards the front of the van to get a better look.

"Paul, you idiot!" She slapped the back of his head. "We're in Cheticamp!"

"Cheti-who?" Wade asked.

"Cheticamp. Dumb-dumb here drove past the turn-off. Why didn't you wake me up if you were lost?"

"I wasn't lost. You said to turn at the Red Barn and keep going," Paul argued.

"I said to follow the signs," Lucy snapped back. "Think about it dumb-dumb... Margaree Valley." Lucy said, emphasizing the word valley. "A valley means between mountains, not next to the damn ocean."

Lucy looked around and saw a field of stick figures dressed in clothes and Halloween masks.

Lucy pointed to the figures, "Joe's Scarecrows."

"Joe's what?" Lauren asked.

"I remember those," Emma said excitedly. "I was here with my parents a few years ago. The whole field is a bunch of scarecrows dressed up with cute little name tags and stuff. The little restaurant over there has great cheeseburgers."

"Oh, my god, Emma!" Lauren shook her head. "Do you think about anything other than food?"

"But I'm hungry," Emma tried to explain.

"You're always hungry," Lauren told her. "For how much you eat you should weigh like five hundred pounds."

"Part of her already does," Paul laughed.

"Ha, ha," Emma said dryly. "Like I never heard that one before. That's about as original as calling someone with glasses four-eyes." As soon as Emma said it, she embarrassingly lowered her gaze to the floor.

"Now that was fuckin' funny!" Paul roared.

Michael smiled as he pushed his glasses back up on his nose.

"Sorry," Emma murmured to Michael.

"That's okay," Michael told her, "all things considered, it was actually kind of funny."

They all smiled.

"Well, at least he didn't keep going," Lucy informed everyone. "Just up ahead is Cheticamp. As soon as you go through Cheticamp, the road leads into Highland Park. If dumb-dumb here had kept going, we would have gone through the Highlands, up along the coast by Meat Cove, down through Neil's Harbour, and back down to Baddeck!"

"Sounds like a long drive," Wade said absently.

"I'll say," Lauren answered. "It's would have been a five-hour round trip to end up exactly where we started. Great driving genius."

"Shut up," Paul warned her.

"So, how far is Margaree from here?" Michael asked.

"Ummm, it's about thirty minutes, I think," Lucy answered then looked at Paul. "In the other direction. That cop was right, you can't read signs."

"I'll drive for a while, Mate," Wade volunteered.

"I can read the signs," Paul argued defensively.

"No worries," Wade reassured him, "you look stuffed."

"I look what?"

Wade laughed. "Tired, Mate, you look tired. I'll drive for a spell and you rest."

They switched seats and Wade turned the van around and headed back the way they came.

Chapter 3 – Beinn Breagh

"Good morning, Robin," Professor Patrick Heslin's voice echoed in his empty laboratory.

"Good morning, Father," a computerized voice responded.

Heslin used his connections, and his check book, to hire the best engineers and developers to build him the Robin-1 computer. A system so advanced that it could do more than just assist him with his research, but it spoke to him as well. Unlike other computer systems, it didn't use a set of canned responses, The Robin-1 Computer had a brain. Officially, it was called artificial intelligence, but the truth was, the Robin-1 Computer was so advanced it appeared to be able to 'think' far outside its primary programming.

Using videotapes from his daughter's twelfth birthday party, the last real birthday his daughter Robin ever had, the engineers and developers not only gave the AI brain Robin's sweet and innocent voice but her angelic face as well, allowing the computer to simulate various facial expressions as she talked. Robin's forever twelve-year-old face filled the computer monitor as Heslin sipped his morning coffee.

"I checked the weather forecast, Father. It is going to be very hot today. Shall I turn on the air conditioner?"

Robin controlled nearly every aspect of Heslin's lab from the satellite uplink and electrical system to the surveillance and security system, including the locks on the doors. Cameras placed throughout the entire building allowed Robin to monitor everything. Speakers and microphones allowed Heslin to talk to Robin from any room inside the building.

"Robin, you know I prefer fresh air from open windows," Heslin responded. "What are the probability results of Formula 25-41?"

"Did you forget, Father?" Robin asked.

"Did I forget what?" Heslin inquired with a hint of a smile breaking across his lips.

"Did you forget what today is?" Robin replied.

Heslin smiled with a wide grin as he looked into Robin's face on the computer.

"Of course not," he said lovingly. "How could I ever forget such an important day? Happy Birthday, Robin!"

Robin's face smiled. Heslin's mind drifted back to his daughter's twelfth birthday; it was a beautiful, sunny day and their backyard was filled with balloons, games, pony rides, and too many screaming children.

Heslin was known to be habitually late for just about everything; important meetings, dinner engagements, Heslin was even late for his wedding. His friends jokingly told him he would be late for his own funeral. But, when it came to Robin, Heslin was never late. He never missed a music recital, a school play, or a single birthday. For her, Heslin was always on time; always there for her.

Heslin, a man years ahead of his peers in the field of genetic research, now resembled a pitiful man talking to a computerized version of his daughter. To an outsider, it would look as though the award-winning scientist had finally gone mad, but to those who knew him well, it was exactly what Heslin needed to keep his sanity. He needed his Robin. Without her, Heslin simply could not go on.

It was only three short years ago that Heslin was working in his lab at the research center when he received an urgent phone call. At first, Heslin understood the words, but as the news grabbed hold, the words became fuzzy, unclear. Heslin's hand released the grip on the phone, the receiver bounced on the desk with a loud clunk. Heslin leaned back in his chair, staring straight ahead. His friend and colleague, Professor Lindsay Paulson, ran to Heslin to see what was the matter as the voice on the telephone handset repeated, "Hello? Hello? Professor Heslin, are you still there?"

"Patrick, are you ok?" Lindsay asked. Heslin did not reply.

"Hello?" The voice on the phone insisted, "Sir, are you still there?"

"Hello?" Lindsay questioned as she put the phone to her ear, "What's going on?"

"Is Professor Heslin all right?"

"Not exactly," she retorted. "What did you say to him? Who is this?"

"This is Sgt. O'Brian. Are you a family member of---"

"This is Lindsay Paulson," she announced, "I work with Patrick. What happened? What did you say to him?"

Tears raced down her face as the sergeant explained that a drunk driver slammed into Mrs. Heslin's car, instantly killing her and sweet little Robin.

"Oh God, no!" she sobbed. Lindsay looked at Heslin, "Patrick, I am so sorry."

Heslin did not answer. He just sat there, staring ahead, a blank look on his face.

As the news of the tragedy spread, Heslin's lab quickly filled with colleagues and lab assistants to try and comfort the grieving man. Eventually the lab cleared, leaving Heslin alone with his sorrow. Lindsay stayed behind to further comfort him and made the obligatory offer:

"If there's anything I can do, Patrick, just let me know."

Heslin lifted his eyes to Lindsay and uttered two simple words.

"There is."

He scribbled on a piece of paper and handed it to Lindsay. Her eyes opened wide in disbelief.

"No, Patrick, do not ask me to do such a thing. You're… you're not thinking straight…. I think maybe you should…"

"Do it!" Heslin's sharp words cut her off. "I don't care what it takes. I don't care what it costs, just do it."

This time it was Lindsay who stared blankly ahead.

Now, three years later, Heslin paced impatiently in front of his microscope, deep in concentrated thought. A thick, grey stubble on his face showed a tell-tale sign that he hadn't shaved in days. His wild, Einstein-like hairdo meant he hadn't showered either.

Heslin often worked to the point of exhaustion, slept for three or four hours, then started another marathon session that lasted for days at a time.

Heslin glanced at his stopwatch as he hovered over his microscope. Impatiently, he switched between staring into the eyepiece and looking at his watch.

The seconds slowly ticked by.

Heslin was an old-school scientist and preferred microscopes and test tubes instead of a completely computerized laboratory. Although everything under the microscope was hooked into the Robin-1 Computer, Heslin still preferred to see it with his own eyes.

Beneath the all-seeing eye of his microscope, a culture dish held reddish-gray cells that moved in a jerky motion when Heslin's genetically modified, translucent green liquid touched the cells. Not really a touch, more like a gentle caress. The reddish-gray cells were human, long since dead, but now sparked with new life when Heslin's translucent green cells caressed them; life that never broke the two-minute window. Heslin dared another look at his watch as Robin's voice broke the deafening silence.

"Formula 25-41 approaching the two-minute mark in 10, 9, 8, 7, 6 . . ."

Robin stopped counting.

Heslin's heart sank as he closed his eyes knowingly and exhaled deeply. He didn't have to look into the microscope to know the cells had stopped moving. He knew exactly what failure looked like. He had seen it too many times before, more times than he cared to count. He opened his tired eyes as Robin started to announce the results.

"Test complete. Sequence has failed. Formula 25-41 not capable of supporting---"

"I know!" Heslin blurted angrily, cutting her off. "I bloody well know. Goddammit! Five more seconds! Is that too much to ask?"

Heslin's question echoed in the empty lab. The last of his assistants had quit weeks ago when Heslin could no longer afford to pay them. Working Heslin's marathon hours was practically suicide, but without the lure of money, his assistants quickly abandoned the maniacal professor.

Living off cold coffee and a few bites of the occasional sandwich, Heslin continued his research, oblivious to the world around him, and to the hunger pains that often growled in his empty belly. His appetite was for something bigger, something monumental and more important than mere food. He was so close to succeeding that he could practically smell victory. Despite his countless defeats, he never flinched in his pursuit. He was determined to prove his theories right... and his colleagues wrong.

The scientific community laughed at him when he first presented his proposal that dead tissue and dead blood cells could be regenerated back into living organisms. He proposed that the dead brain cells of Alzheimer's patients could be brought back to life. Heslin even dared to suggest that loved ones lost in terrible accidents could be brought back to life.

Knowing of his recent loss, his peers thought his intentions were "misplaced." Others had simply labeled his ideas as Frankenstein-ish, and although none would admit it, many feared that if he did succeed, the end result would not be that much different than the monster in Mary Shelley's famed novel.

Rage filled Heslin's already exhausted mind as the sound of mocking from his peers crept back into his memory. He grabbed the beaker of Formula 25-41 and fired it across the room. The beaker exploded against the wall just a few inches above the opened window. The loud crash of shattering glass snapped him out of his rage. Heslin laughed in spite of himself.

"Well now, Paddy me boy, that was rather dumb now, wasn't it? Now you have a mess to clean up."

"Father, is everything all right?" Robin asked.

"Not now, Robin," Heslin answered abruptly, looking at his watch.

6:10 a.m.

Quietly, Heslin grabbed a small garbage pail and began to pick up the broken shards of glass as the thick, translucent green liquid succumbed to gravity and slowly oozed down the wall.

His mind lost on his recent failure, Heslin grabbed a piece of broken glass the wrong way. A sharp pain jolted him back to the task at hand. Blood poured from the deep cut. Instinctively, he put the cut to his mouth. He knew it didn't really help the pain, He knew that it was just a psychological link to when his mother had the power to heal hurt with a loving kiss, but he sucked the cut anyway.

Overcome with disappointment, yet clinging on to a fragile hope, he peered inside the microscope's eyepiece once more. Nothing moved.

He adjusted the magnification as a small trail of blood trickled down his cut finger.

A solitary drop of blood hung suspended from his hand, daring to fall.

In less than a heartbeat, the tiny drop of blood began its descent. It splashed in the culture dish, hardly noticeable to the naked eye, but under the magnification of his powerful microscope, the tiny splash looked like a giant wave of red reaching up to grab him. Startled, Heslin quickly collected his thoughts and looked at his hand. Blood was streaking down his forearm.

"I have to stitch this," Heslin said to himself as he headed out of the laboratory.

Robin spoke up. "Father...."

"Not now, Robin."

"Father. . ." she repeated.

"Go to sleep now, Robin," Heslin commanded, cutting her off.

The computer monitors instantly went black.

The command, "Go to sleep now, Robin" was a built-in fail-safe known only to Heslin and the programmers of the Robin-1 Computer. Robin prevented everyone, Heslin included, from accessing her AI brain so that no one could tamper with her programming. The command was created so Robin could be shut down to allow for routine maintenance of the system. At the end of a one-hour period, a second fail-safe timer automatically rebooted the main system, turning Robin back on.

Heslin hissed in pain as he fumbled about trying to stitch the deep gash on his finger. The folks down the mountain may have called him Doc, but his feeble attempt to stitch his wound proved he knew very little about practical procedures. He was a scientist after all, not a medical doctor.

Heslin thought about the good folks in the Valley, hardworking people who welcomed the scientist with open arms and, as he requested, left him alone so as not to disturb his research. Once a month they ran supplies up to him, mostly by 4-wheel drive, but during the harsh winter months, a snowmobile was the only vehicle that could make the trip up the secluded mountain road.

Perched on the mountainside, he sometimes felt like his idol, the great inventor, Alexander Graham Bell. Bell had settled in the nearby village of Baddeck, not more than an hour's drive away. Heslin proudly hung a picture of Bell above his mantle. Below it, a plaque displayed Bell's immortal words:

"I have traveled the globe. I have seen the Canadian and American Rockies, the Andes and the Alps and the highlands of Scotland, but for simple beauty, Cape Breton outrivals them all."

Sitting on the mantle above a giant fireplace was an old fiddle that had once belonged to Heslin's father. Occasionally, when he needed to clear his thoughts, Heslin would play the old fiddle, but that was a rare occasion as he was usually too busy working in his lab, trying to perfect his formula. The rest of the pictures in the massive lounge area were all of Robin. There was one old wedding photograph with a much younger Heslin and his pretty bride, but the other pictures were of his sweet, little Robin.

Heslin hoped to acquire some of Bell's inspiration by building his lab on his own *Beinn Breagh*, which was Gaelic for *Beautiful*

Mountain. Gaelic was a dying language on the island, save for a few small communities buried deep in the highlands. Heslin understood some of the Scot Gaelic words and he marveled at the fact that Scottish musicians often traveled to the island to learn the Cape Breton style of fiddling, which remained practically unchanged by time. Cape Breton fiddling was said to be closer to original Scottish fiddle music than in Scotland itself.

On a quiet summer night, Heslin could sometimes hear the faint sounds of a fiddle, carried by the warm summer breeze. Other times, he heard the majestic drone of highland pipes. Both were music to his ears and a welcomed distraction.

Heslin's lab, controlled by Robin and filled with modern equipment, was a stark contradiction to Bell's modest laboratory, forever captured in time at the Bell Museum located in the village of Baddeck, a place Heslin occasionally visited for inspiration. Unlike Bell's modest lab, Heslin's was a sterile, clinical white, lit by huge florescent lights and flickering computer monitors. He had everything a modern laboratory needed. Well, almost everything.

At first, just like all his junior lab assistants when they first arrived on the mountain, he too had been taken aback by the sheer size and beauty of the old lodge standing proud on top of the mountain with a million-dollar view.

The spruce and pine trees seemed to hug the giant log building as if the lodge was meant to be there. It was beautiful and breathtaking. And, just like his assistants, he quickly grew to hate the fact that this kind of beauty and seclusion had a very steep price: modern conveniences, or lack thereof.

No cable, no phone, and no running water except for a small electric pump that drew water from an outdoor well, and worst of all, no proper toilet. An outhouse stood ten yards from the back door and proved to have two major flaws: In the summertime, the smell was absolutely disgusting and burned your nostrils with the putrid smell of feces as it baked in the summer sun. During the harsh winter months the smell wasn't nearly as bad, but sitting on the cold, hard plastic seat left a lot to be desired.

When the construction of the lab was completed on the main lodge, Heslin had planned on installing proper facilities, but with the lab ready, every day a new idea or a new experiment took hold and pushed further renovations aside.

Now, three years later, Heslin still used an old diesel generator as backup power for the lodge; the main power was supplied by massive solar panels.

A temporary hot water shower was installed in one of the upstairs rooms by running rows of copper pipes across the roof. In the summertime, the sun baking the pipes on the black shingles provided them with all the hot water anyone could ever need, but in late autumn the pipes had to be drained so that they would not freeze and burst, which meant everyone was forced to settled for sponge baths instead of hot showers.

Solar panels supplied enough electricity to keep the lab warm during the winter, but Heslin had to manually pump water from the deep well because the subzero temperatures of a typical Margaree winter froze the waterline, and every winter he still had to freeze his ass off in the outhouse. Heslin hated that outhouse. He hated it so much that some days he prayed for constipation just so he would not have to go to that disgusting place. But his steady diet of cold coffee made sure that prayer was never answered.

With his hand freshly wrapped in too much gauze, Heslin headed to the lounge area and poured himself a scotch. He swallowed it in one drink then refilled his glass. Distraught with failure, he flopped in the big Lazy Boy chair and stared at the picture of Bell hanging above the fireplace. He took another drink, stood up, and walked towards the picture.

"Well Mr. Bell," he said to the picture, "now what do I do?"

Heslin stared at the picture as if he was waiting for an answer. The picture said nothing. Heslin gently picked up his father's old fiddle and tucked it under his whiskered chin. He fumbled with the bow, the gauze on his hand making it difficult to tighten the bow or properly hold it. With a soft, quiet breath, Heslin gently pulled the bow across the strings.

The once quiet room was now filled with sound as Heslin played the old Scottish tune, "Neil Gow's Lament for the Loss of His Second Wife".

Playing the tune always seemed to clear Heslin's cluttered mind and soothe his feelings of failure. As he played, Bell's picture seemed to take on a new look.

The picture itself never changed, only Heslin's perception of it. In his mind, Bell seemed to smile in appreciation.

Birds and crickets seemed to appreciate it as well, for their singing became louder, drifting in the open window in harmony to Heslin's playing. The sound of the little creek that flowed just a few feet from Heslin's lab before traveling down to the valley also seemed to bubble just a little bit louder. A symphony of nature joined the gentle sounds of Heslin's fiddle.

As he played, Heslin's mind drifted back to a time three years earlier when he'd sat looking across a large, oak conference table with the twelve men he had invited to hear his proposal. They were all wearing tailored suits and expensive watches, obvious signs of wealth. Each knew of Heslin's recent loss, but when a Nobel Prize-winning scientist requested a meeting, especially one whose last proposal had generated a huge return on investment, only a fool would not attend that meeting.

It was at this meeting the potential investors quickly learned Heslin's new proposal was far beyond anything they could have ever imagined.

Chapter 4 – The Proposal

"So what you are saying, Professor Heslin," one of them finally broke the cold silence that swallowed the room, "is that you want to bring the dead back to life? Sounds more like science fiction than a business investment."

Several chuckles followed. Heslin stood abruptly, silencing the chuckles. His thick, wavy hair, once a rich brown, was now a bright shade of gray and made Heslin look older than his forty years. He stared intently at the man for the briefest of seconds, but it was enough to make the man shrink back into his chair. Heslin broke his piercing stare then looked at the men with smiling eyes as he began the speech he had prepared for exactly this moment.

"Science fiction. I've heard that before," Heslin's lips curled into a boyish smirk. "From scientists no less."

The men smiled with him, the tension in the room slowly subsiding.

"Gentlemen," Heslin continued in a commanding voice, "I could go on and on about how the mere thought of being able to hear a human voice across hundreds of miles on copper wires was thought to be mere science fiction, yet Bell created his telephone. And let's not forget Marconi. Sending the sound of a human voice across the ocean without any wires! Preposterous!"

Heslin paused a practiced pause, scanning the eyes of his audience.

"How many inventions have we witnessed since their time? Artificial hearts, computers, satellites, cellular phones… the list of science fiction becoming a reality goes on and on."

Heslin paused as he pulled a tiny locket from his vest. He opened it carefully, glanced at it, and smiled. None of the men dared interrupt him.

"I'm sure everyone in this room believes it is the death of my little Robin that is fueling this project."

The men nodded hesitantly.

"It is." He snapped the locket shut. "No parent should have to bury their children."

He let that thought linger in the air then turned his attention to the man to his left.

"John, you know exactly how I feel. You lost a child less than a year ago, is that correct?"

"Yes," John answered. "Anna. She died of leukemia."

"She was only seven years old, wasn't she?" Heslin softly asked with sympathetic eyes. It was a redundant question, Heslin had done his homework. Not only did he already know the answer, he handpicked each of these dozen men for a specific reason, a reason other than their check books.

John nodded.

"Imagine," Heslin said as he slipped the locket back into his pocket, "that somebody could have waved a magic wand and given you your Anna back. What would you be willing to give to be able to hold her again?"

John didn't have to think what he would give, his answer came immediately, "Anything. Everything."

"Anything and everything," Heslin repeated John's words slowly. "In fact, I believe every man in this room has a child. Imagine for a moment if your child was snatched from your life like Robin was snatched from mine, or Anna from John's. What would you give to have your child back? To have the power to be able to hold your precious, sweet and innocent child in your arms once again?"

All eyes focused on Heslin, hanging intently on his every word as he picked up his proposal.

"Gentlemen, I do not have a magic wand," he slammed the written proposal on the desk, startling the twelve men. "And I don't deal in science fiction! When I succeed…"

Heslin shifted all his weight to one foot, a trick he learned that resulted in naturally deepening his voice by almost a full octave to place more emphasis on his next sentence, "and I will succeed. Each and every one of you will have that power."

Heslin could see he had their interest, so he turned their attention to the more practical applications of his proposal. He understood men like this well enough to know that "practical application" to them meant making money.

"While medical centers around the world struggle to meet rising organ demands, we will have the power to all but eliminate the need for organ donors. We will have the power to repair and revive the patients' own organs!"

Heslin sat back in his chair, clasping his hands behind his head.

"My colleagues think I am a madman." Heslin smiled. The men smiled with him.

"Oh yes, they think I have completely lost my mind." he paused with a devilish smile. "Of course, they said the exact same thing right before I won the Nobel Prize. People live, people die, accidents happen, and diseases kill. Such is life."

Heslin leaned forward. "Yet despite all our medical advancements, these tragedies continue to happen. Why do we allow our loved ones to die needlessly when we could have the power to change all that? We will have the power to add years to someone's life, or even bring back a loved one from an untimely death. And..."

Heslin ended his performance with one final pause, then added a practiced smirk, "with this power we will be able to charge whatever the market will bear."

He let his last sentence hang in the air. Life was a beautiful commodity to sell, and with hundreds of thousands of people not quite ready for death, the market would bear a lot.

As the men talked amongst themselves in hushed whispers, Heslin swore he could see dollar signs in their eyes. It was only a few minutes before the men unanimously decided to invest in his unique and rather bizarre proposal. It was a gamble to say the least, but if anyone could pull it off, they knew Heslin had the drive and expertise to do exactly that.

And, if he did succeed, they would be far beyond the mere cutting edge of science, they would be reinventing it, and making more money than they could ever imagine. They agreed to fund his research for the next three years.

When the last of the men left the room, Heslin pulled the tiny locket from his vest pocket once again and lovingly stroked the picture.

"Soon," he whispered to the picture. "Soon."

The clouds that cluttered Heslin's mind dissolved and a new spirit took hold. He remembered the mess he'd made in the lab so he promptly returned his father's old fiddle to its case, grabbed his scotch, and headed back to the lab.

He stopped at the microscope to dispose of the ruined culture dish when, like a young boy who finds his father's Playboy Magazine, he just had to look. He leaned over the eyepiece and instantly bolted up straight, dropping his glass of scotch. It bounced on the floor, throwing the scotch at Heslin's feet, but the heavy glass did not break.

It rolled to a stop as Heslin, wide-eyed, fumbled with the sleeve of his lab coat and stared at his watch.

6:49 A.M.

The corners of his mouth turned up in a tiny smile. Heslin dared another look. This time he stared more intently into the eyepiece. Again he stood up straight, his tiny smile now replaced with a wide, foolish-looking grin.

"We did it, Robin!" He announced proudly. "We did it! The formula works!"

Heslin danced around his lab in joyful hysteria, completely oblivious to the translucent, green liquid oozing out the open window.

Tracks of green ran down the outside of the lodge, pooling into a green puddle. But gravity wasn't quite finished with Heslin's green liquid...

Not yet.

Gravity pulled the liquid out of the little pool and down the sloped landscape, swerving around tiny rocks, following the path of least resistance. At the head of the green trail, a tiny drop of Heslin's creation was poised over the edge of the small creek, threatening to jump.

It just sat there, like a nervous diver too scared to take the final plunge. Another bubble of green raced down the last incline and slammed into the timid diver, pushing it over the edge. It hit the creek with the tiniest of splashes, barely creating a ripple, and began its long journey to the valley below.

Heslin danced around his lab in triumphant victory, but his dance was cut short by a sharp pain in his stomach. A few seconds later, the pain subsided. As he stood up, he noticed the open window and the green stain above it.

Heslin raced to the window. He looked out at the little, green trail leading towards the creek.

"Robin, run an analysis on formula 25-41 and it's interaction with fresh water."

Robin did not respond.

"Robin," he said again. "I need you to run an analysis on…."

Heslin scratched at his bandaged hand, remembering that he had shut Robin down. He banged frantically at the keyboard but the system did not respond.

"I need to reboot the system. I need Robin to…."

Another crippling pain dropped Heslin to his knees. He screamed in agony as the pain came in waves. When it ceased, he pulled himself back to his feet.

"I have to reboot the system," he said to no one as he started to unwrap the gauze, his hand burned with a powerful itch.

Another intense pain struck him down again. When that wave of pain subsided, Heslin crawled towards the back door, a trail of gauze following him.

"I need air," he panted as he staggered outside, deeply inhaling the fresh air.

Heslin gritted his teeth and hissed in pain as he finished unwrapping his hand. Wide-eyed he stared at it as shock and fear raced through his mind. His entire hand was a gray and purple color; it smelled of sour cheese and baby vomit. The finger he had cut was blackened as if some type of advanced gangrene had set in. He tried to wiggle his fingers but they refused to move. He thought about the tracks of the formula leading to the creek.

"My God, what have I done?"

Chapter 5 – Margaree

The van pulled to a stop at the Irving station at the Inverness turnoff.

"Why are we stopping?" Michael asked.

"We need petrol," Wade answered. "You pump in twenty bucks worth. I'll go pay." He looked at the price. "A buck forty-five a litre! Christ," Wade said sarcastically, "that's bloody highway robbery. How do these cockies afford to live up here?"

Wade walked inside the station. "Oy?"

No one answered.

"Paying customer here, Mate?"

Still no answer.

"For what you are charging for petrol you should be out there pumping that crap yourself!" His voice echoed off the concrete walls.

"I'll leave some moolah on the counter, all right?" Wade yelled as he slipped the twenty back into his pocket. "Stupid nongs," he laughed as he walked back to the van, jumped in, and drove away.

Just over the next hill, a neon "Open" sign on the local co-op grocery store caught Lucy's eye.

"Stop here," Lucy ordered.

"For what?" Wade asked.

"Duh, for some food. There won't be anything to eat at the cabin."

"Food is good," Emma agreed. "I'm hungry."

"Of course you are, " Lauren rolled her eyes.

Wade spotted the Nova Scotia Liquor Commission sign on the side of the Co-op building and slammed on the brakes, jolting the gang forward. "Good idea, grab some grog too."

"Grab some... what?" Lucy asked

"Some beer," he answered.

When the group walked into the store the first thing Michael noticed was that there weren't any people; no customers wandering the aisles, no staff stocking shelves or standing at the cash registers. It was eerily quiet and still.

"Hello?" Lucy yelled. "Is anyone here?"

"Christ," Wade asked, "is this some holiday out here in the back of beyond?"

"What do you mean?" Lucy asked.

"Same thing back at the servo. Nobody around," Wade answered.

"Hello?" Lucy yelled again. This time they heard a noise.

"See," Lucy told him, "they're out back, probably having a meeting or something."

"A meeting. Yeah, that's it." Paul laughed. "A meeting as to why shit keeps getting stolen." Paul yelled in the direction of the store-room door, "It's because you leave everything unattended for people to steal ya dumb hicks."

"Knock it off," Lucy elbowed him in the ribs. "Let's go see what's going on. Maybe somebody's hurt."

"What are you, a doctor?" Paul asked sarcastically. "Let's just leave the money on the counter and get the hell out of here. This place creeps me out."

"I'm with you, Mate," Wade agreed, pulling out some money. "Screw it!" He said with a grin, putting the money back in his pocket. "Let's just go."

Paul and Wade headed for the door.

"Assholes," Lucy shook her head in chagrin as Wade and Paul left with a case of beer.

"I'll go with you," Michael offered, following Lucy to the back of the store.

Lauren watched the scene without saying a word as her friends scattered in different directions, leaving her standing alone in the unnaturally quiet store.

Emma walked around the corner from one of the aisles holding a couple bags of potato chips.

"What's going on?" Emma asked.

"Nothing," Lauren answered. "Let's go."

"What about these?" Emma asked, nodding towards the bags of chips she was holding.

"The hell with the chips. Let's go." She grabbed Emma by the arm and started to lead her out the door.

"But I'm hungry," Emma pleaded.

Lauren threw a five-dollar bill on the counter. "Take the damn things. Now c'mon. Let's go."

Lucy and Michael approached the door to the back of the store slowly and cautiously, a byproduct of watching too many horror flicks. They gently eased the door open a little and was greeted by what sounded like gnawing sounds.

They opened the door a little more. The back room was dimly lit, but it was enough to see what looked like an employee kneeling over something on the floor.

"Hello?" Lucy asked sheepishly, barely louder than a whisper.

The employee didn't move.

"Hello?" Lucy said again, slightly louder. "Is everything Ok?"

The employee turned his head then paused. He was motionless as if trying to decide if he really heard someone. Lucy noticed the employee's mouth was covered in blood as he continued to chew. Lucy's breathing quickened as she lowered her eyes to what he was holding in his hands. A bloodied arm.

Lucy's eyes widened; her heart pounded in her chest as she looked back to the man's face. He opened his mouth for another bite and a partially chewed finger fell to the floor.

Lucy screamed. The employee turned towards her and let out a weird, groaning yell.

Lucy stood frozen in horror as Michael pulled on her elbow. Another employee appeared from behind a stack of boxes, chewing on a human leg, then let out the same groaning yell.

Michael pulled Lucy through the door, dragging her to a run. They raced out of the store and towards the van.

"Go! Go! Go!" Michael yelled as he pushed Lucy into the van.

"What's wrong?" Wade asked as Michael slammed the door shut.

"Go!" Michael yelled again.

Wade raised an eyebrow questioningly, then looked towards the Co-op store.

Two blood-soaked people wearing Co-op aprons staggered slowly out the door; one still chewing a half-eaten arm.

"Christ!" Wade yelled as he floored the accelerator, jolting his friends back into their seats.

Michael quickly looked out the back window at the grotesque employees and noticed they barely flinched when Wade showered them with rocks - they just kept walking towards the van. They didn't run, they just slowly staggered slowly towards the van.

"Holy shit!" Wade repeated several times as the speedometer continued to climb. The van went over a steep blind crest, lifting all four tires in the air.

"Slow the fuck down!" Paul yelled, "before you kill us! Who the hell were those people?"

"They were… eating… people!" Michael responded slowly, more to himself.

"They were eating people?" Lauren and Emma asked in unison.

"What the fuck kinda hillbillies live here?" Paul asked as he looked in the rearview mirror.

"Something's wrong," Lucy mumbled to no one in particular, her eyes still wide in disbelief.

"No shit, Sherlock!" Paul growled. "How the fuck do we get to your cabin?"

"Something's wrong," Lucy repeated.

"Oy! Bambi!" Wade yelled. "We know that already. How do we get to your bloody cabin?"

Lucy did not answer. Wade cut the wheel hard to keep from going off the road, then slowed to a more manageable speed.

As the van raced along the winding, country road Wade spotted a few dozen cars parked by a building next to a church.

"Oy, car park up ahead is full."

"Thank God!" Lauren answered. "Civilization!"

Wade pulled into the parking lot as the tires crunched in the thick gravel. The large community center that sat next to the church didn't show any signs of activity. They all stared at the quiet building skeptically.

"Somebody has to go check," Wade suggested.

"You go check," Paul said as he moved to the back to sit with Lucy.

"I'm driving!" Wade answered.

"My heroes," Lauren said as she shook her head in disappointment, "big on muscles, short on courage."

She opened the van door, looked in the direction they had just come, and cautiously stepped out of the van. She looked back at her friends. Nobody moved.

"Y'all just gonna sit there and let a girl go by herself?"

Michael swallowed a lump in his throat.

"I'll go with you," he said as he stepped out of the van. "Wade, keep the door open and the engine running."

Wade nodded in agreement.

Michael turned to Lauren, "All right then, let's go."

Emma jumped out of the van. "I'll go too."

The three friends looked once more in the direction they had come, then back at the van where Lucy rocked back and forth in Paul's arms mumbling, "Something's wrong. Something's wrong. Something's wrong."

They hesitantly walked towards the door of the building. The sign on the door read, "St. Patrick's Ceildh. Admission: Good Will Donation."

They stared at the sign.

"Awfully quiet for a party," Emma said as she pulled the door open.

The stench hit them like a slap in the face. Bodies covered in blood lay everywhere. Emma and Lauren covered their mouths to keep from gagging.

Michael noticed that not everyone was lying on the floor; some were kneeling over the bodies, just like at the Co-op. One of the kneeling people was a little girl who didn't look to be more than ten years old. Her angelic face was covered in blood.

Emma noticed it first. "Is she eating a…"

Lauren finished her sentence. "A baby. Oh my God, she's eating that baby!"

Emma let out a piercing scream. The little girl turned to face them, still chewing. Michael heard the same groaning yell from the little girl. The rest of the people in the hall suddenly stopped eating and looked straight at the three friends standing in the doorway.

"We gotta go! Now!" Michael shouted as more of them emitted that groaning yell. He pulled on the arms of the stunned girls as the people in the hall started to move towards them.

"Run!" he shrieked, dragging them out of the doorway.

They raced across the parking lot as a hoard of blood-soaked people flooded out the door, walking towards the van in the same unsteady swagger as the employees from the Co-op.

Emma was still screaming uncontrollably as Michael shoved her into the van. Wade floored the accelerator. The tires spun in the deep gravel.

"Go! Go! Go!" Michael yelled.

"I'm fuckin' trying!" Wade yelled back as the tires finally grabbed hold and the van peeled onto the road.

The sound of screeching tires briefly drowned Emma's screams. Michael watched the people barely flinch as they were showered with rocks. The van fishtailed down the road as Wade tried to bring it under control.

"It's like they don't even feel pain," Michael mumbled to himself as the van sped away.

Paul returned to the front seat and looked at Wade who shrugged his shoulders. He didn't know what in the hell was happening either.

Emma's screams were replaced by a steady stream of tears and sobbing. Lauren looked as if she was about to throw up. Michael looked like Michael always looked. He had that weird, dazed but concentrated look on his face, the kind people get when they run into somebody they know and their name is right there on the tip of their tongue, but they can't quite say it. That's the look Michael had on his face.

"Turn at the fork in the road," Lucy announced weakly.

"Look who's back," Paul said sarcastically. "Welcome to Margaree. I hope you know coming here was your fuckin' idea!"

"Leave her alone," Michael glared at him. Paul stared back.

"Don't look at me with your macho, He-man bullshit," Michael argued, "we've got bigger problems right now than your stupid jealousy."

Paul said nothing. No one said anything. They all knew Michael was right. They did have bigger problems. Bigger than anything they could ever have imagined.

"Christ!" Wade yelled as he slammed on the brakes and lurched everyone forward in their seats.

They all stared out the front window. A small child, maybe only six or seven years old, was standing on the road next to a crashed car, her tiny mouth covered in blood.

"She's one of them. What do I do?" Wade asked.

Paul stared at the little girl, then answered in a slow, monotone voice, "Run her the fuck over."

"What?" Lauren yelled. "She's just a child."

Paul spun his head glaring at her. "She's just a child that eats people!" He turned back to Wade. "Listen to me. Those fucking things are everywhere! We can't stay here waiting for little miss I-want-to-eat-your-fucking-heart to get out of the way. So floor it and run her the fuck over!"

Wade looked back towards the others. They lowered their eyes to the floor. They all knew Paul was right, but none of them wanted to say it out loud. Wade looked back to the little girl staggering towards them.

He floored the accelerator.

"Move kid," Wade mumbled. "Come on kid, move."

She didn't move.

Wade closed his eyes as the van slammed into the little girl with a sickening thud.

"Fuck!" Wade cursed, his eyes watering up. "Why didn't you move?"

"Ho-ly shit!" Michael said as he looked out the back window.

"What?" Wade yelled back.

"She got up!" Michael answered.

"She what?"

"She got up!"

Wade looked in the rearview mirror in disbelief. The little girl was on her feet, walking towards them as the van sped away.

Wade said the only thing he could think of saying, "What the hell do these people put in the water?"

Chapter 6 – The Cabin

"Turn here," Lucy announced.

The van skidded to a stop then turned left towards Centre Margaree. They crossed over Cranton Bridge, a popular swimming area and salmon fishing spot on the Margaree River, but nobody was swimming or fishing today.

Ahead of them was another gas station. They didn't stop for gas. They made a right and headed towards Portree Road. The road dipped up and down like a roller coaster. It looked like it hadn't been paved in twenty years. At one turn, the edge of the road had caved in where the Margaree River pounded into the side of the mountain for hundreds of years until it finally collapsed the road above. They could see a long stretch of the Margaree River in all its majestic glory. It was a million-dollar view, but right now the only view they wanted to see was Lucy's cabin. Wade navigated the turns cautiously.

They crossed a small bridge that opened into a large, flat valley when Lucy spoke up.

"It's the little red place on the left."

Michael noticed a few other houses and cabins around, but no people. He wasn't sure if that was a good thing or not. The van drove up the grassy driveway then rolled to a stop. The hot sun was starting to set as the gang jumped out of the van and ran towards the cabin.

Lauren turned to Lucy. "Do you have the keys, Lucy?"

"No," Lucy answered.

Everyone looked at Wade.

"What? Oh I get it, all of a sudden I'm a B&E expert. I'm insulted."

"Can you get us in or not?" Lucy asked.

"Of course I can," he answered with a smile, "but I'm still insulted that everyone assumed I could."

He walked up to the door and rattled the doorknob.

"So, who has the lock picking tools?"

They all looked at him but said nothing.

"Guess it's plan B then," he said as he stepped back and kicked the door below the handle.

The door frame shattered as the door flung open.

"After you, ladies," Wade motioned to the door.

"I could have done that," Paul said as he shook his head.

"Ahh, but you didn't. I did," Wade answered with a smile.

"For your next trick," Paul added, pointing to the splintered door frame, "I want to see you lock it again to keep those things out."

Paul was still grinning as Wade pushed past him.

"You people expect me to think of everything," he mumbled and turned back to Paul. "Instead of standing there grinning like a dill, go grab the tinnys."

"Grab the what?" Paul asked.

"Tinnys. The cans of beer."

Paul looked towards the van. Michael stood in the waning light and stared silently at the hilly mountains that surrounded Margaree Valley.

"Hey star gazer, door's open."

"Looks like there's a light up on that mountain," Michael yelled back.

"Yeah, so? We're down here, not up there. Grab the beer!" Paul ordered as he stepped inside the cabin.

Michael grabbed the cooler of beer and walked towards the cabin.

"Something tells me we should be up there," he thought out loud.

Inside the cabin Lucy flicked the light switch. Nothing. She flipped the switch for the main power breaker. The lights flashed to life for the briefest of moments. Darkness enveloped the cabin once again.

"Damn Fuses," she announced. "there has to be more here somewhere."

They helped her search for spare fuses in the failing light, but without any success.

"Guess we're camping in the dark," Emma said as she turned on the tap.

Nothing came out.

"It's an electric pump," Lucy informed her. "No electricity, no water."

"Any other good news?" Paul asked. "We don't have any electricity, there's no water, and look," he pointed to the old stone fireplace. "No wood to build a fire. Nice place you brought us to, Lucy."

"Hey, guys," Michael spoke up, "we can't stay here."

"Why not?" they all asked in unison.

"This place is too open. We don't have any electricity. There's no food or water...." Michael started.

"Hey, I have water!" Lauren announced. "Two or three bottles in my duffel bag."

"There's six of us," Michael told her. "And we don't know how much longer we'll be stuck here. A couple bottles of water and some beer ain't going to help us much. I don't see anything we can use to board up the windows and," he looked at Wade, "the door won't lock."

"Well, I didn't see anyone else coming up with ideas," Wade bit back.

"If we find a rope and a bucket," Lucy suggested, "We could get some water from the well."

"We could," Michael said, not really agreeing with her. "But that means fumbling around out there in the dark. Not the best plan."

"It's not," Paul reluctantly agreed. "We should just stay here the night and head for St. Peter's in the morning. Who in the hell were those people?"

"Zombies," Emma said to herself, not realizing she said it out loud.

"What?" she asked when she realized everyone was staring at her.

"She's right," Michael suggested.

"Oh please," Paul spoke up. "Zombies? Gimme a fuckin' break."

"No, think about it," Michael tried to explain.

"Think about what?" Wade interrupted. "This ain't the movies, Mate."

"No, it's not," Michael answered. "Those things out there are very real, and they are headed this way."

"You don't know that!" Paul argued.

"Then let's go by what we do know," Michael suggested. "We saw them eating human body parts."

"I hate to break it to you, Sherlock," Paul interrupted, "but that would make them cannibals, not zombies."

"Perhaps," Michael continued. "But when we ran out of the Co-op, and out of that hall, they didn't run after us. They walked. They staggered. Like they had no coordination."

"So?" Wade questioned.

"So, when you pulled away," Michael told him, "twice I saw you shower them with rocks, and twice they barely even flinched. It was like getting pelted with rocks didn't even hurt them! And," Michael added, "what about the little girl you ran over?"

"What about her?" Wade asked.

"You hit her doing what? Forty, fifty miles an hour? We all felt the van hit her, then she got up! That impact should have killed her, but she got up and started walking after us! I don't know what they are or how they got that way, but everything so far points to zombie-like behavior."

"Is there a point to all this?" Lucy asked.

"My point is," Michael answered, "is we can't stay here."

They all stared at him, not knowing how to process what was actually happening."

"When we first saw them Lucy," Michael continued, "you said 'hello' but they didn't really hear you until you screamed. It wasn't until that first one made that weird growling sound that the other one showed up."

The gang stared at him, still trying to process the information.

"And at the hall, they didn't even know we were there. But as soon as Emma screamed, that little kid let out the same type of growl, and that's when the rest of them looked. We all know what zombies are like from the movies and these people are behaving the same way. It's like their brains can't really distinguish one sound from the next, but that growl they make... it's like some kind of sensory communication... or something."

"Sounds kinda weird to me," Wade said sarcastically.

"And people eating people or little girls getting up when they were hit by a van is not weird?" Lauren asked.

"They didn't really see or hear us," Michael explained. "But as soon as one of them knew we were there and made that growl, they all knew we were there."

"Then that settles it," Paul announced. "If we stay here in the dark and be real quiet, they won't be able to see or hear us."

"No," Michael explained, "think about it. If they don't hear that well and don't see that well, how do they find food?"

"How?" Emma asked, even though she was pretty sure she didn't want to know.

"By smell." Michael let his words sink in before continuing. "They must be able to smell food."

"Then why didn't they smell us when we opened the doors?" Lauren asked.

"I don't know," Michael answered. "That place reeked from all those dead bodies. Maybe that smell was so strong it hid our smell. It's starting to get dark and we don't have any lights. We won't be able to see them coming. They could be right outside the door and we wouldn't even know it."

They all looked at the shattered door.

"We're sitting ducks here," Michael told them. "Even if we did see them coming, you saw how the tires spun on the thick gravel, and now the sun is going down. That means the temperature is dropping. That means we'll be spinning our tires on wet grass trying to get away. It's not safe here."

"Where do you suggest we go?" Lucy asked.

"We can't go back the way we came because there's too many of them on the road. I don't think the van could plough through them all. I saw lights on top of one of those mountains. That means there's somebody up there."

"What if there's not?" Lauren asked.

"Then at least we know there's electricity. Lucy, do you know what that place is?"

Lucy looked out the window in the direction Michael was pointing.

"There's a hunting lodge up there. My dad said some doctor bought it a few years ago."

"A hunting lodge means guns," Michael stated.

"Oh great," Paul interrupted. "Stay here and get eaten or go up there and get shot! Great plan."

"No, he's right," Lucy said, "If someone is up there, I don't think they expect those..." she hesitated then said reluctantly, "those zombie things to drive up in a van."

"What if they are... zombies too?" Emma asked.

"It's pretty secluded up there," Michael explained. "We didn't come across any of those things coming into the valley, so it should be safe up there."

"Should be!" Paul laughed. "That's comforting."

"I think we should do what Michael says," Lucy suggested.

"Oh, I see how it is," Paul said sardonically. "Everything lately is Michael and Lucy. Where you go, he goes. What he says, you agree with. Something you guys want to tell me?"

Lucy shot Paul a dirty look.

"Grow up. You're such a dick."

"I'm telling you guys, we have to get out of here," Michael continued, ignoring Paul's jealous comment. "We are surrounded by houses and cabins and God knows what else. If one of them senses we are here, how long do you think it will take before more of them answer that weird growl they do?"

None of them answered.

"We know they don't move very fast," Michael added. "So the quicker we get out of here, the better."

Michael looked impatiently at his friends. To him, it seemed like it was taking forever for them to make up their minds, but it was reality it was only a few seconds.

"Ok, then," Wade said, half smiling. "Let's head up to the top of the mountain. That way we'll be closer to heaven when we die."

Lauren laughed. "If that's the case Wade, you're going in the wrong direction."

Everyone chuckled nervously as they headed out the door.

Michael noticed a butcher block and grabbed a large kitchen knife. As he turned towards the door he spotted a large machete hanging above the door. He dropped the kitchen knife and pulled the giant machete out of its sheath imitating Crocodile Dundee, "That's not knife. Now that's a knife."

Wade poked his head back in the door, smiling. "I heard that!"

Michael returned the machete to its sheath, stuffed it in his backpack and followed his friends to the van.

As Wade pulled onto the road they noticed people covered in blood were coming out of their houses. They were all walking in that same unsteady swagger. They were all walking directly towards the van.

"They're all coming out at the same time. I wonder why?" Emma asked.

"We are why," Lauren answered. "It's feeding time."

Chapter 7 – Big Ben

Wade swerved around as many of them as he could. He knew if the van took too many hits it could crack the radiator, or they could get hung up on one of them. Being outside on foot with those zombie things was not something any of them wanted to experience. A few minutes later they passed the last of the small horde. Michael looked out the back window and watched them slowly follow the van.

"Just like before," Michael said to no one in particular, though everyone was listening intently. "They're following us."

The van crawled up the steep, rocky road as the sun fell behind the mountains, blanketing them in darkness.

"For Christ's sake!" Wade said shaking his head.

"What is it?" Paul asked.

"We left the esky back at the cabin."

"We left the what?" Paul asked.

"The esky."

"What in the hell are you talking about?"

"Doesn't anyone in Canada speak English?" Wade asked sarcastically. "The cooler. We left the bloody cooler of beer back at the cabin."

"Smooth move, Exlax," Paul snickered. "Want to go back for it?"

Wade slammed on the brakes.

"Jesus Wade, I was kidding!"

"Shut up!" Wade whispered. "I thought I saw something."

Everyone looked. Wade flicked on the high beams, and that's when they saw it. A huge, black bear moving onto the road and walking towards them.

"Holy shit!" Emma said, too loud for everyone's liking.

"Shhh!" Lauren warned her.

The bear stopped in front of the van, staring directly at Wade. Wade's heart pounded in his ears, his arms started to shake uncontrollably when the bear stood on its hind legs directly in front of him. A cold sensation raced down the back of Wade's neck and shoulders. His breath came in short bursts.

Wade saw two giant paws with terrifying claws thud down on the hood of the van. Wade froze, too afraid to even look away. He could not speak. The claws lifted and thudded down again, shaking the van. Its roaring breath blew spit on the windshield.

"Now what do we do?" Michael yelled over the girls' screams.

Paul looked at Michael. "You distract him so we can drive around him."

"Yeah, right. I'll get right on that."

"No, seriously, Mikey," Paul told him, "slide open the door and lean out. When it sees you, it will go to the side of the van and then we can drive past him. I'll pull you back in."

Michael looked at Paul doubtfully, "Pull me in? You'll probably throw me out."

"Listen," Paul snapped back in an irritated voice, "this is fuckin' serious, man. You said those zombie things are following us, and Big Ben there is blocking the road. We can't wait for him to move, so we have to lure him out of the way."

The bear stood on his hind legs again and roared.

"His eyes are all fucked up," Wade said to no one in particular. "He's a goddamn zombie bear."

"Why me?" Michael asked Paul timidly.

"Would you prefer I hang one of the girls out the door instead?"

"No," Michael replied uncomfortably.

"Wade is driving, and I'm stronger than you. I can pull you back in quicker," Paul told him. "So that leaves you."

Michael swallowed a lump in his throat.

"Michael," Paul said, placing his hand on Michael's shaking shoulder, "it's no big secret that you get on my nerves, and sometimes I'd like to kick the shit out of you, but like you said, right now we got bigger problems. And right now, our biggest problem is that fuckin' bear. You have to trust me."

Michael looked at Lucy. Lucy looked at Paul, then back to Michael and slowly nodded.

"Somebody do something!" Wade's voice cracked.

"Give me your belt!" Michael said to Lucy.

Michael looped her belt around his wrist and offered the other end to Paul. He forced a smile, "Paul, if you let go, I will kick the shit out of you."

Paul smirked and wrapped the belt tightly around his wrist.

"I won't let anything happen to you," Paul promised.

Lucy took a deep breath and slid the door open. Michael hung out of the side of the van, holding on to the belt for dear life. Michael yelled at the bear. It looked at Michael for a brief moment then turned his attention back to Wade.

Michael picked up a rock and threw it. The rock bounced at the bear's feet, but the bear still didn't move.

"Big Ben doesn't like your plan." Michael tried to sound brave, but his shaky voice told the truth.

He threw another rock. This time it hit the bear in the head. The bear dropped to all fours, let out a blood-curdling growl, then moved towards Michael.

"Now!" Michael yelled.

Paul pulled Michael in and Lucy quickly slammed the door shut. The bear stopped. It stared at the side of the van, then turned its attention back to Wade.

"Umm, guys," sweat was running down Wade's forehead, "he looks really pissed now, like he wants to come through the windscreen. Do something!"

The bear opened his mouth and roared. Wade could see the bear's giant, yellow teeth in the moonlight. Wade's hands continued to shake uncontrollably.

"Shit!" Michael nodded to Lucy. "Open it."

Lucy slid the door open again. Michael leaned out.

"Over here you overgrown furball!" Michael yelled.

"I'm sure that'll hurt his feelings," Paul said as he shook his head.

"Fuck you," Michael answered without taking his eyes off the bear. He picked up another rock to throw but the bear dropped back to all fours and moved towards Michael.

Paul pulled Michael back in so forcefully he almost dislocated Michael's shoulder. Lucy slammed the door shut just as the bear slammed itself into the side of the van. The impact lifted two wheels off the ground. Everyone screamed in panic.

Wade floored the accelerator.

The van bounced the gang around like rag dolls as Wade raced to get away from the monstrous killer.

They screamed for Wade to slow down, but he was driving like a mad man; like a man possessed. He was possessed, with fear.

Sheer panic had grabbed Wade and wasn't letting go.

The van bounced around another sharp corner as it raced up the rocky mountain road. The rear tire slammed hard into a large boulder that knocked the air out of the tire. It threw the van into an uncontrollable turn.

The van raced off the road, slamming hard into a giant tree.

The impact threw Lucy so hard against the front seat that it punched her breath away, then instantly slammed her back into her seat as the van crunched to a stop.

The impossibly loud screams of terror and shattering glass shrieked in her ears as something heavy slammed into the back of her head, pushing her down onto the hard, metal floor.

The faint but steady hissing sound broke the silence as the radiator's steam escaped into the still, night air.

Lucy tried to get up but something heavy pinned her down. Was Lauren on top of her? Lucy's mind, numb with fear and shock, struggled to form a single thought. It wasn't Lauren on top of her, it was Lauren and Emma.

"Get off me," Lucy exhaled sharply as she awkwardly tried to push them away.

They didn't move; their combined weight was too heavy.

"Get off me!" she pleaded in a shaky voice.

A claustrophobic feeling of being trapped raced through her aching body. With one last adrenaline-fueled push, she broke free of the web of tangled girls, then shook them violently.

"Wake up," she tried to yell, but it sounded more like a whisper as a buzzing sound built in her ears.

She steadied herself and took a few slow, deep breaths to keep from passing out.

She heard the girls make a soft moaning sound, so she crawled towards the front of the van, first shaking Michael and then Paul. The hissing sound grew faint as the last of the steam was released from the crumbled radiator that hugged the giant tree.

Lucy's eyes widened with terror when she looked at Wade. The windshield directly in front of him was shattered. It looked like a million tiny spider webs weaved and crawled away from a large, crimson-rimmed hole. The top of Wade's head disappeared into that hole.

It only took a few seconds for Lucy's still-numb brain to put the pieces together. Wade's head did not disappear into the hole; his head made that hole.

Panicked, she tried to pull Wade free from the spider web. The windshield released its grip on him with a wet, sucking sound as Wade's head popped free. As he fell back into the driver's seat, his head slumped to the right. His eyes, wide with shock and pain, looked directly at Lucy. His hair clung to his forehead, matted down with glistening red. Tiny speckles of glass dotted his bloodied face like red glitter.

"Lu..cy?" Something liquid and gurgling roughened his voice.

Lucy felt another stab of panic. She mouthed his name, but she could not squeeze out enough air to make an actual sound. Tears raced down her cheeks in a stream of sadness and fear.

"L-Lucy," Wade repeated in a fragile voice.

Globs of blood gurgled over his quivering lips. Lucy took his hand and held it to her wet cheek. His eyes were glassy; unfocused. She choked out a pathetic sound that resembled his name, but her tears were too strong, her breath too weak, for any coherent language.

She gently squeezed his hand. He did not squeeze back. As the rest of the group groaned painfully back to consciousness, Lucy was kneeling quietly by Wade's seat, still holding his hand to her tear-soaked cheek.

"Wade!" Paul yelled, panicked, as he scrambled toward his friend.

"Wake up! Wake up, buddy!" He tried to shake him awake but Wade did not move.

"He's...he's gone," Lucy sobbed as she knelt on the floor and held his lifeless hand.

Paul shook him again and yelled, "Fuck!"

Lauren let out a piercing scream; Emma threw up. Michael wiped a tear away with the back of his hand and slid the door open. "C'mon," he told them. "We gotta go."

"Go? Go where?" Paul yelled. "We're not going anywhere without Wade. We can't leave him here. We can't leave him like...like this!"

Michael grabbed Paul by the arm. "Paul, listen to me. That bear will be here any minute. Those zombie things are on their way. We have to go. Now!"

"Not without Wade," Paul yelled as he jerked his arm from Michael's grip. He moved back to Wade and started to drag him out of the van. "I'm not leaving him here for... for them! He's not a piece of meat!"

Michael laid his hand gently on Paul's shoulder. Michael's voice, soft and gentle whispered, "He was my friend too."

Paul stared blankly at Michael.

"We'll close up the van," Michael told him, "so nothing can get in. When we get to the hunting lodge and get the guns, and some help, we'll come back for him."

Michael's voice deepened as it took on a more commanding, almost monotone sound.

"But right now Paul, we need to man-the-fuck-up and get the hell out of here."

Paul didn't say a word as he inhaled deeply and stared at Michael. A few deep breaths later, Paul nodded and set Wade back into the driver's seat as gently as if placing a baby in a car seat, then stepped out of the van to join his friends. He slammed the door shut then scanned the distraught and horrified faces of his companions.

Michael had watery eyes; the girls were still crying. Paul took a slow and deliberate breath then said in a dry, matter-of-fact voice, "Okay boys and girls... let's get this walking feast moving."

A loud crack echoed in the still night.

The girls screamed. An instant later, the rain came. It pounded the group, drenching them in coldness.

Paul looked skyward and yelled, "Can you please give us a fuckin' break?"

Chapter 8 – Strangers

"Good evening, this is Clay Buffer with the Atlantic Television Network's 6 o'clock evening news. Tonight's top story: A series of bizarre murders in the tiny village of Margaree Valley has authorities baffled. Chief Brian Dunn of the Royal Canadian Mounted Police refused to make a formal statement pending further investigation. Sources close to the Chief claim the RCMP have blocked all roads going in and out of the Margaree Valley area, and they're working around the clock on the tragedies that have besieged the isolated community since early this morning. Field reporter, Jess Jessup has the story."

"Thank you, Clay. We have just received reports that members of the CDC have been flown in from Atlanta, Georgia, along with members of the American National Guard to assist the RCMP and the Canadian Armed Forces as they quarantine the area. Some startling new evidence has led officials to believe that some type of virus has infected the residents, causing them to attack their neighbors, friends and families."

"Excuse me Jess, did you say a virus is causing people to attack their own families?"

"Yes Clay, that's right. A virus."

"Is this virus causing some type of massive paranoia or psychosis? I mean, they're attacking their own family. What exactly is this virus?"

"At this time, the CDC is not releasing any information. No discernible motive has been established as of yet, but sources have suggested the murders are horrific and beyond anything they have ever seen."

She paused as a man dressed in an expensive suit handed her a piece of paper. Jess held up her finger to ask for a brief moment to read the note.

"The official liaison for the CDC has just informed me," Jess then read out loud, "that they will be holding a formal press conference tonight at 10 P.M., Atlantic Standard Time. The virus is not airborne and is contained within the Margaree River Valley area. The rest of the island is not in any danger of infection."

Jess hesitated as she re-read the last piece of information on the paper. She looked up at the camera, then hesitantly lowered her eyes. For the first time since she became a journalist, her voice wavered as she continued to read. "Authorities are warning citizens that anyone attempting to leave the Margaree area will be dealt with swiftly and severely."

Jess looked into the camera again. Her mouth opened but she had no words.

"Thank you Jess," Clay quickly responded to kill the dead air. "That was Jess Jessup reporting from outside Margaree on Cape Breton Island. More on that story later tonight on the Late-Night News. And now, the weather forecast---"

###

"Father?" Robin's voice echoed in the empty lab.

Various rooms flicked on and off her screen in rapid succession. To the human eye, the screens were little more than a blur. But to Robin, she easily scanned every nook and cranny of each room that her camera-lens eye could see.

The images on the monitors rapidly changed from the interior cameras to the security cameras mounted on the outside the lodge. The screen froze on a small group of people walking towards the lodge. As the group stepped into the light, Robin scanned the individual faces of these uninvited guests. She searched her memory banks. This group of people was unknown to her. The locks on the door clicked shut as the strangers stepped onto the huge veranda and a hand reached for the doorknob.

"It's locked," Lucy said as she jiggled the handle.

"Hello?" she raised her voice as she knocked on the door. "Is anyone there?"

She waited a moment, listening intently, then pounded the door harder.

"Hello! We need help! Somebody open the goddamn door!"

The computer monitors flashed in rapid succession again, still searching the rooms. Once again the images stopped on the security camera that was focused on the strangers. Unable to find Heslin, Robin's only course of action, the most logical one, was to allow these strangers entrance to help her search the places her camera eyes could not see. If Heslin was hurt, these strangers could administer medical aid, something else she was unable to do.

Robin sensed something in her system she never sensed before. It was a new process, outside her primary programming. It felt like... but it couldn't be...

Robin knew that was impossible...

Computers could not feel.

Robin's artificial brain could duplicate various preprogrammed expressions to simulate feelings, but they were only simulations. Somehow Robin knew this was different. This was new. She was... *scared*.

The locks on the door clicked open as her monitors went black.

Lucy pounded the door again and tried the doorknob. This time the knob turned. She hurriedly pushed the door open; a large, empty foyer welcomed them. The group rushed into the lodge and quickly locking the door behind them.

"Hello?" Lucy yelled again.

No answer.

She turned to Michael and Paul. "Check upstairs."

She turned her attention to Lauren and Emma. "Check the kitchen, check..." she paused for a moment, "Just check everywhere. The door didn't unlock itself, so somebody has to be here. Everyone meet back here in five minutes."

Paul looked at her, slightly puzzled and rather annoyed.

"Who the hell put you in charge?"

"You did!" she snapped back.

"What did I do?"

"Not a damn thing," she answered as she turned her back to him and walked away.

"What the hell is that supposed to mean?" he yelled after her, but she ignored him and disappeared around a corner.

Michael patted him on the shoulder. "It means you didn't do anything when we walked in here, so she did."

Paul's face still held a puzzled look as Michael headed upstairs. Lucy stood in silent awe of an all-white room filled with computers and laboratory equipment. This was something she never expected to see in an old hunting lodge on top of a mountain. She knew everyone referred to the new owner as 'Doc' but this was beyond anything she could have imagined for a doctor.

"We're not in Kansas anymore Toto," she said to no one as she spotted the open window and hurried over to it. She noticed the weird greenish colored stain above the window then quickly pulled the window shut and locked it. The rest of her friends soon found her in the lab.

"What the fuck is this place?" Paul asked as he entered the bright lab.

"Good question," Michael answered absentmindedly as he took in the surroundings, admiring the computers.

"I need a drink," Lauren said as she turned and headed for the kitchen.

"I need a hot shower and get out of these wet clothes," Emma announced.

"Something's not right," Michael thought out loud.

"Let's see," Paul smirked. "We are in the middle of fuckin' nowhere in some sort of secret laboratory with flesh-eating zombies outside. Seems about right."

"Wait!" Michael yelled, running to the kitchen. The others quickly followed as Michael yelled to Lauren.

"Don't drink that!"

Lauren hesitated just long enough for Michael to pull the glass away from her open mouth. He tossed it into the sink, shattering the glass.

"It's only water," Lauren explained.

"Listen, what do you hear?" Michael asked.

Everyone froze and listened intently.

"Don't hear a damn thing," Paul told him.

"Exactly," Michael said bluntly. "Other than that bear, we didn't see or hear anything. No other animals. No birds, no crickets… nothing."

"So?" Lauren asked.

"So we are in the middle of the forest on top of a mountain and we can't hear a damn sound?"

"Enough with the cloak and dagger bullshit," Paul answered. "Just tell us what in the hell you're talking about. What do birds and crickets have to do with Lauren having a drink of water?"

"This place is deserted, and there's some type of high-tech lab here. I don't know what the hell happened to the people up here or down there in the valley, but the only way for anything up here to get down there is through the water."

They looked at him, not quite fitting all the pieces together.

"Don't you get it?" Michael motioned with his hands as if it should be obvious. "Water runs downhill. So I think whatever happened up here somehow got into the water and caused all that shit down there."

"Oh, that's just fucking great!" Paul said. "It was your bright idea to come up here, and now you're saying that this is where it all started?"

"I don't know if it started here," Michael admitted. "I just know we can't take any chances until we figure it out."

"I think he's right," Lucy told everyone.

"Oh, look," Paul snorted sarcastically. "She agrees with him. There's a shock."

Lucy rolled her eyes and tried to ignore Paul. "Follow me. I want to show you guys something."

They followed Lucy into the lab. She pointed to the window.

"That window was opened when I got here. And look, there's some sort of stain above it."

"Yeah, so that stain could have been there for years," Paul said.

Michael looked out the window then pushed it open again.

"Way to go, Einstein," Paul yelled to him. "Open the window so whatever's out there can get in!"

Michael ignored him as he leaned out the window, his eyes following a tiny, green trail down the side of the building, then off into the darkness.

"I can't really tell," he informed them as his eyes reached the end of the light cast from the window. "It looks like a trail of that stuff leads down to a creek over there. So maybe whatever leaked out the window did get into the water." Michael thought for a moment then amended his statement.

"That has to be it. It's the water."

Paul was not convinced. "Water runs downhill, so we have nothing to worry about up here now do we?" He looked at Michael, "Or should we all just die of thirst because you think you might be right?"

Emma nodded towards the computers.

"Maybe we can find out what they were working on."

They moved towards the computers, but just as Emma's hand hovered over the keyboard a voice startled them.

"I would not do that if I were you," Robin warned.

"Who the fuck said that?" Paul jumped back with fists closed as his eyes searched the lab. Michael reached for the machete in his backpack. A moment later the monitor turned on, revealing Robin's face.

"What the...?" Paul leaned towards the monitor, studying the computerized face as its eyes moved from person to person, then looked directly at Paul.

"My name is Robin. Have you seen my father?"

"Your father? Is this some kind of sick joke?" Paul asked as he stood up straight and looked around the lab.

"Shut up, Paul," Lucy said as she waved him off. She turned back to the monitor and asked, "Who is your father?"

"Professor Patrick Heslin," Robin's eyes turned towards Emma, her hand still hovering above a keyboard, "and he will be very angry with you if you touch that keyboard."

Emma pulled her hand back.

"For Christ's sake Emma," Paul said as he shook his head. "It's just a computer program."

"What happened here?" Lucy asked.

"What happened? Are you serious?" Paul asked. "It's a computer. How in the hell is it supposed to know... why in the hell are you even talking to it?"

Lucy waved him off with another gesture to be quiet.

"My name is Robin."

"You said that already," Paul said sarcastically. "Not a very smart computer either."

Robin's eyes seemed to focus on Paul.

"The Robin-1 Mainframe controls all the electrical and electronic components of this laboratory," Robin's eyes narrowed on Paul. "And you were not invited here... Paul."

"What the...?" Paul was stunned to hear Robin speak his name.

Robin turned her attention to Emma. "Your name is Emma."

Robin looked at the others. "I do not know your names."

"This is stupid," Paul cut her off. "So it remembers names, big fuckin' deal. So now we're supposed to introduce ourselves to a stupid machine?"

"Artificial Intelligence," Emma announced. "I've read about it, but never realized that it could be so complex."

"Me either," Michael agreed. "They don't have anything like this in the computer club."

"It's artificial, all right," Paul smirked then headed for the main house. "Maybe there's some booze or something to drink." He looked at Michael, "Since we can't drink the water."

"Good old Paul," Michael laughed. "Even in the face of danger, he insists on being an asshole."

"I heard that!" Paul's voice sounded from the next room.

"I was not sure of your intentions," Robin informed them as she looked back to Lucy, "so that is why I did not make my presence known when you first arrived. I had to be sure you meant no harm."

"So what happened here?" Lucy asked again. "I'm Lucy, by the way. That's Michael, and this is Lauren."

"It is my pleasure to meet you," Robin smiled as she looked at them, then turned her attention back to Lucy. "I do not know what happened. We were working on the experiment and then---" Robin stopped.

"And then what? What experiment?" Lucy asked.

"I am not permitted," Robin replied. "Have you seen my father?"

"No, we haven't. Not permitted to what? We need to know what happened here."

"If you find my father, he will be able to explain everything to you," Robin answered.

"I already told you," Lucy argued, getting irritated. "We don't know where he is. What experiment?"

"I am not permitted."

"Arrgghh!" Lucy exhaled in frustration. "Of all the computers in the world, we get the stubborn one!"

Lucy took a deep breath.

"Ok, Robin, here's the deal. We'll help you search for your father, and then you explain to me what experiment you were working on."

"My father will be able to---"

"Not your father," Lucy cut her off. "you! You agree to explain everything, and we will help you find Professor Heslin."

Robin was quiet for a moment and then spoke. "Your proposal is acceptable."

"Ok, guys!" Lucy said to her friends as Paul returned carrying a bottle of scotch. "We need to do a complete sweep. First, make sure all the doors are locked."

"The doors are locked," Robin informed her.

"And the windows...?" Lucy asked.

"The locks on the windows are mechanical. I do not control them."

"So what's the point of controlling the door locks if anyone can just break in through the window? That doesn't make much sense." Paul smirked.

"No, it does not," Robin answered.

A second later they heard a loud rumbling sound as a massive steel shutter closed over the laboratory window. Another loud rumbling sound followed and a steel door slid from behind a wall and slammed closed. It locked with a metallic thud.

"The laboratory is now completely sealed," Robin announced. "Is there anything else you wish to comment on, Paul?"

"Ummm, nope. I'm good," Paul replied sheepishly.

"Robin," Lucy asked, "are all the windows sealed with these shutters?"

"I can only secure the laboratory," Robin explained. "My father was only concerned with the security of the laboratory due to the nature of his work."

"Which was what?" Lucy asked.

Robin smiled.

"It was worth a shot," Lucy said, then smiled at Robin.

"Okay Paul," Lucy turned her attention to her friends. "You check the rest of the house and make sure every window is locked. Lauren, check the fridge and cupboards and find out how much food is here, and see if there's any bottled water. Emma, go upstairs and start checking the rooms, and look for Professor Heslin."

"What about me?" Michael asked as Robin opened the steel door.

"Check the cellar for wood and tools to board up the rest of the downstairs windows. For how uncoordinated they walk, I doubt those things can climb up to the second floor, so they should be ok for now. We should get the lower level secured first, then worry about the upstairs.

"Smart. I'm on it," Michael said and quickly disappeared.

Lucy started looking around the lab for clues as to what had happened. Notebooks, scraps of paper, anything. She spotted the microscope sitting on a worktable and moved towards it when she heard Michael yelling to her from the cellar.

"Hey, Luce... I think you should come take a look at this."

She hurried down the cellar stairs as Paul made his way back to the laboratory, still carrying the bottle of scotch. He looked at a row of small monitors and noticed each one had a numbered label that started with the word CAM. He flicked the switch for CAM-1 and a room appeared on one of the monitors.

"Cool," he mumbled under his breath.

One by one he flicked on the monitors. Some were of the kitchen and living room; a couple of monitors showed the grounds surrounding the lodge. Paul stared at CAM-9. He watched as Michael and Lucy were standing in the basement staring at a huge, steel door. Paul watched them intently on the tiny screen. Neither of them moved. He flicked the switch for CAM-10. It was one of the rooms upstairs. He saw Emma looking inside a closet. He watched as she pulled a shirt off its hanger and tossed it on the bed, her back to the camera.

"Now this is more like it," Paul muttered as Emma turned just enough so he could watch her undo the tiny buttons of her wet shirt.

Paul had no idea why someone would install a camera in a bedroom, but right now he was thankful they had. When the last of her buttons were undone, Emma paused as if she could feel someone's eyes watching her. She turned towards the door. It was still closed. She held her shirt together and walked to the door, walking out of the camera's line of sight.

"Damn!" Paul said, disappointed, his eyes still glued to the tiny monitor.

He quickly glanced at CAM-9. Lucy and Michael hadn't moved; they appeared to be talking about something. Paul turned his attention back to CAM-10.

Emma opened the door and looked into the hallway, peering both left and right. Empty. She closed and latched the door before returning to her previous position by the tiny bed as her shirt flowed behind her. Paul licked his lips in anticipation.

Paul watched excitedly as Emma pulled her arms through the sleeves and let the shirt fall to the floor. With a move few men can understand, Emma reached behind her with one hand and unclasped her bra. How women could do that so easily, and with only one hand, was beyond him. Emma's wet bra fell to the floor, her breasts now in full view.

"Nice tits," he whispered, then quickly looked around the lab to make sure he was alone before turning his attention back to the small monitor.

Paul's gaze was so focused on Emma's naked torso on the CAM-10 monitor that he didn't even see the group of shadowy figures appear on CAM-6 as they slowly staggered towards the lodge.

Chapter 9 – The Cellar

Lucy looked around the cellar; piles of old junk, broken furniture, rusted tools, and dusty, old boxes lay everywhere. Next to the steel door, a computer monitor sat silent, its dusty screen blank. Lucy looked into the blank screen.

"What's behind that door Robin?"

Silence.

"I know you can hear me Robin. What's behind the door?"

Robin's face appeared on the dusty monitor. "It is only storage."

"Only storage, huh?" Lucy asked, not believing her. "Then open it."

"I am not---" Robin paused for the tiniest moment, "Able."

"You're lying," Lucy told her. "Open the door."

"Lying?" Michael asked. "Computers can't lie."

"This one can," Lucy answered.

"There is nothing of interest behind the door," Robin stated.

"Then why are you here?" Lucy asked matter-of-factly.

Michael hid a smile as Lucy continued to question Robin.

"If this is just a dusty old cellar filled with junk, then why did the Professor take the time to install a camera and monitor?"

Robin did not answer.

"Robin, you said your father was only worried about the security of the lab, so why install a steel door and a security camera in a damp and dusty old cellar that's only used for storage?"

Robin still did not answer.

Lucy waited then asked, "Robin, can you see inside that room?"

"I am not able to see inside the room," Robin answered immediately.

"But you know what's in there?" Lucy asked, not expecting an answer. Robin didn't give her one.

"What if…" Lucy said with a mock look of fear, "what if your father is in there?"

Robin's face on the monitor took on a more concerned look as Lucy continued her charade. "What if he's hurt? We can't help him if we are locked out here and he's in there hurt."

Lucy tried her best to sound sincere. She wondered if she would be able to trick Robin into opening the door.

Michael nodded approvingly with the hint of a smile. A moment later, the silence that enveloped the dusty cellar was broken by the sound of a loud, metallic click.

Michael pushed on the steel door and it groaned open.

Michael and Lucy stepped through the door into a long, narrow room lit with a lone incandescent bulb suspended from the ceiling. Directly below it sat a large, stainless-steel canister with tubes and wires that ran to a nearby computer terminal.

Unlike every other computer monitor that they had seen so far, Robin's face did not appear on this computer; Robin watched them from outside the steel door.

Michael nudged Lucy and pointed to the far corner. A dozen or so steel cylinders labeled "Liquid Nitrogen" stood in the corner. The entire room was lined with steel walls; the stainless-steel canisters gleamed against the all-gray room. A solitary chair sat next to a canister labeled 'LifeCorp'.

"What is all this?" Lucy asked, turning to the doorway to see Robin's face on the dusty monitor. Robin did not answer.

Lucy read the label on the big, stainless-steel canister, "LifeCorp."

"LifeCorp?" Michael asked.

"That's what it says."

"LifeCorp," Michael repeated. "That name sounds familiar."

Lucy looked back out the door and saw that Robin was watching them.

"Robin, what's all this stuff for?" Lucy asked.

"I am not permitted," Robin's voice echoed through the open doorway.

"Of course not," Lucy mumbled under her breath.

"I remember!" Michael announced excitedly. "LifeCorp. I read about them in one of my dad's old Sports Illustrated magazines. Some baseball player died years ago… Jimmy something… Jimmy 'Fastball' Williams. He died and they froze him."

"They froze him?" Lucy asked incredulously.

"Yeah. His family was arguing over how his remains were supposed to be disposed of. Some wanted a burial, others wanted cremation or some nonsense like that. Anyway, they had LifeCorp freeze the guy until their lawyers sorted it all out but his skull cracked. The family was pissed. It was a big scandal"

"That would explain the liquid nitrogen," Lucy said, more to herself, as she looked back to the LifeCorp canister.

"Yeah, it's called Cryogenics," Michael told her.

"Cryogenics," Robin spoke up, "is the study of the production of very low temperatures and the behavior of materials at those temperatures. Cryogenics is often used incorrectly to refer to cryonics, which is cryo-preserving humans. It is a common mistake."

Lucy looked at Michael and whispered mockingly, "It is a common mistake."

Michael smiled and rolled his eyes.

"So," Lucy said in a more serious tone, "Now that we know what this crap is for, the big question now is who's it for? Who's in the canister Robin?"

"I am not permitted," Robin answered.

"Listen little-miss-I-am-not-permitted," Lucy snapped irritably. "How do we know that the Professor is not in there? You're a computer… the Professor could have been dead for years and you wouldn't even know." Lucy paused for a moment, "I'm tired of your games. Who's in the damn canister?"

"I am not per---"

"Yeah, yeah, yeah, you're not permitted! Listen here you little computer bitch… either you tell us who's in there, or we're just gonna have to pop this sucker open right now and have a little look-see for ourselves!"

"You are not permitted to do that!" Robin answered quickly. "If you open the capsule without following the proper procedure it will destroy…" Robin paused. "It will destroy the cells."

"Well that's a chance I am willing to take," Lucy said as she drummed her fingers on the canister. "It's not like we are hurting anyone; they're already dead. And since you won't tell us who's in there---"

"I am," Robin answered.

"What?" Michael and Lucy asked in unison.

"I am in the canister."

"What do you mean?" Lucy asked.

"When I was twelve there was an automobile accident. I died. My father placed me in cryonic preservation. The project we were working on…" her voice trailed off, as if thinking, "he was trying to discover a way to reanimate me."

"Reanimate you?" Michael asked. "As in bringing the dead back to life?"

"That is correct," Robin replied.

"That sounds just a little too farfetched to…" Michael's voice trailed off as his mind grabbed hold of the idea. Secluded laboratory, re-animation, green liquid spilled into the creek, zombie-like people eating other people. Robin broke his train of thought.

"I implore you," she begged, "please do not open the canister or all will be lost."

"You're still here; she's still in there… so it didn't work, did it?" Lucy said, more of a statement than a question.

"No, it did not," Robin answered.

"*I think it did,*" Michael thought as a cold chill raced down his spine.

Chapter 10 – Testing Your Theory

"Good evening, this is Clay Buffer with the Atlantic Television Networks Late Night News at 11. Tonight's top story:

"A sudden wave of violence has struck the quiet village of Margaree Valley early this morning. When RCMP officers discovered the remains of a still yet to be identified female, the RCMP originally surmised the woman was the victim of a vicious bear attack. The partially devoured body was examined by the Sydney Medical Examiner, and he concluded that the bite marks on the victim were not of an animal, but rather, by humans. Several humans.

"Further study of the remains discovered an unknown virus and the CDC was immediately flown in from Atlanta, Georgia, to spearhead the investigation. Our field reporter, Jess Jessup has the story."

"Thank you, Clay. The recent string of cannibalistic slayings and the disappearance of the Margaree River Valley residents have local authorities at a loss. The entire population of approximately nine hundred residents has all but vanished. So far, the RCMP has found the remains of approximately three hundred forty-seven residents in various locations, with the largest cluster of victims located in the community hall of St.

Patrick's Parish. The CDC has confirmed in a press conference earlier this evening that an unidentified virus found in the victims may be causing some residents to attack other people in a cannibalistic nature. However, at this time they are unable to confirm that assessment.

"With the exception of the bodies already found, authorities have been unable to locate any of the other residents. The RCMP has set up roadblocks on all rural roads leading to the foothills surrounding the Margaree River Valley. In addition, the Canadian Armed Forces, with the assistance of members of the American National Guard, are planning a full sweep of the entire area. The highlands of Margaree cover approximately three hundred square miles. Details on the sweep will be released at a later date. Jess Jessup, ATN Evenings News."

"Thank you Jess, and now the weather forecast---"

###

Lucy and Michael ran out of the cellar when they heard Emma's scream.

Paul appeared from the lab and followed them up the stairs with Lauren only a few steps behind. They reached the room Emma was in, but she said nothing. Her shaking hand pointed towards the window. Cautiously, Michael moved towards the window, unsheathing the giant machete as he looked out.

"Damn things are everywhere!" Michael told them.

The rest of the gang moved towards the window and peered outside.

"Holy shit!" Paul whispered. "There's so many of them. Maybe they'll just keep going past us?"

"Anything is possible," Michael said quietly. "Maybe we should all stay really, really quiet… just in case."

"Thought you said they didn't hear very well?" Paul asked.

"I said we don't know what in the hell those people are, and I didn't think they could hear very well, but let's not take any chances just the same. Let's all quietly go back down to the lab where it can be sealed by Robin, and we'll all keep really quiet and see what happens."

Sitting on the laboratory floor, with the windows secured by the massive shutters, the tiny group of friends sat motionless as the sounds of moaning slowly circled the lodge. The hours ticked by painfully slow. Outside, the people banged and scraped at the lodge and boarded-up windows trying to get in.

Everyone's nerves grew thinner as the scrapping gnawed at that patience.

Michael stood up, as he had done several times before, and quietly disappeared upstairs, only to return a few short minutes later. As he took his place with his friends, they all looked at him expectantly. He reported in hushed tones that from the upstairs window it looked like there were at least four or five dozen of those zombie-like things circling the lodge, looking for a way in.

Michael stood and announced, "I'm pretty sure those things hunt by smell. We have been super quiet for hours and none of them are leaving. That means they must be able to smell us."

Paul stood up and stretched his arms. "So we can talk now?"

"Yeah, I guess so," Michael shrugged.

"Thank fuck, I was getting a little batty sitting there. So they can smell us, eh?"

"It appears that," Michael responded.

Paul scrunched up his face, then smiled a few seconds later.

"Oh, my God!" Lucy's eyes watered as she covered her nose.

Paul laughed. "Just thought I'd give them something to smell."

"But did you have to try and kill the rest of us?" Lauren asked. "What in the hell did you eat?"

"Beans, beans, good for your heart. The more you eat, the more you---"

"That's it!" Michael said excitedly.

"Huh?" Was all the rest of them could say.

"Smell. They are attracted to smell."

"Here we go again," Paul said as he rolled his eyes. "More cloak and dagger nonsense."

"Listen," Michael explained, "if our smell is what is keeping them here, then our smell can distract them."

No one made a sound. Their minds were lost in the maze that was Michael's logic.

"This time I have to agree with Paul," Lucy said to break the silence. "What in the hell are you talking about? Why don't you just talk in plain English?"

"Smell," Michael repeated as if it were obvious.

The look on everyone's face proved it was not that obvious.

"Yeah, yeah," Paul mocked, "I smell, you smell, we all smell. So what does smell have to do with anything?"

"Those zombie things are not too bright," Michael explained. "They have been wandering around outside for hours, banging into crap because they can smell that we are in here, but they don't know how to get in. If we can change how it smells in here, and somehow get our smell out there, that will distract them long enough for us to escape."

"Great plan," Lucy said. "But escape to where?"

Am apprehensive silence filled the lab again.

"Ok," Michael said as he lowered his eyes to the floor, his excitement waned. "So maybe it's not a perfect plan, but at least it's something. Maybe we don't have anywhere to escape to right now, but if we can just get those damn things away from here we could all get a little bit of our sanity back."

Paul grinned at Michael, "Getting a little frazzled are we, Mr. Cloak and Dagger?"

Michael ignored his comments and slumped back down on the floor.

"Hey, Emma?" Paul said.

"What?" she replied weakly.

Paul looked at her for a moment. He could tell she was more than just a little frazzled by all this. They were all worried and scared, but Emma looked like she was ready to snap. She was a complete mess. Paul knew that now was not the time for silly blonde jokes.

"We're going to be all right," he said with a smile as he sat next to her and put his big arm around her shivering body. "You hang in there, okay?"

She nodded with a sob and buried her face in his chest. Lucy sat on her other side, rubbing Emma's shoulder to soothe her.

"Thank you," Lucy whispered soundlessly as Paul stood up to stretch his legs. He nodded a smile as Lauren took his place next to Emma to help comfort her.

As the hours passed, all sense of time eluded them. In today's modern world of cell phones and text messaging, wristwatches had become all but obsolete, a relic of a not so distant past, worn more for nostalgia than practicality. A relic not worn by anyone in this group; their trusted cell phones sat somewhere in a smashed van halfway down the mountain.

A loud bang, like a gunshot, pierced the silence and startled everyone to their feet. Another loud bang sounded as they ran upstairs to find Paul aiming a rifle out the window.

"What the hell are you doing?" Michael yelled.

"Testing your theory," Paul answered.

"What in the hell is that supposed to mean?" Lucy asked him.

"Boy genius here said these things are like zombies."

"What does that have to do with scaring the hell out of us?" Lauren asked.

"Mikey said all we have to go on is what we know, right?" Paul explained.

"And...?" Michael asked.

"And… what do we know about zombies?"

"What are you going on about?" Lauren asked.

"In the movies, the only thing that kills them is a blow to the head, right? So, I shot one of them fuckers right between the eyeballs."

"You shot him? Are you insane?" Lucy said disgustedly.

Paul ignored her. "Dropped him like a sack of shit."

"Can you please refrain from your colorful and juvenile descriptions and get to the point," Lauren demanded.

"Second shot was a chest shot, " Paul explained. "The impact dropped him, but he got back up. The headshot guy didn't get up."

"Interesting," Michael thought out loud.

"Interesting?" Lucy said as she stared at Michael in disbelief. "He's shooting people and all you can say is 'interesting'?"

Another shot startled Lucy. She spun around to watch Paul reload.

"Stop it!" she yelled. "They are still people!"

"Those zombie mutha-fuckers are not people! They're the reason Wade is dead!" he yelled back at her. "They ain't human."

"Neither are you," Lucy screamed then ran downstairs.

The other girls quickly followed. Michael stayed behind.

"Where'd you get the gun?" he asked.

"I saw this old 4-10 shotgun hanging above the door in the kitchen. It looked like it was in good shape, and there were some shells in the drawer, so I thought I'd test it out."

"On zombies?" Michael asked.

"Didn't see any rabbits running around, did you?"

"Point taken," Michael said as he looked out the window. "In fact, we haven't seen any animals other than that damn bear. No birds---"

"And no crickets," Paul finished Michael's sentence. "You made your point."

Michael scanned the area until he found the zombie lying on the ground."

"Jesus Paul, you damn near took his head clean off him. That must be one helluva powerful rifle," Michael said as he looked back to Paul.

"What? This? Not really," Paul told him. "Good for rabbits or pheasants, but not much else."

"Well, it sure made a mess of him," Michael nodded towards the downed corpse.

"Yeah, I guess they can move around and stuff, but the body is decaying."

"Interesting," Michael said more to himself than to Paul as the sun peeked over the horizon, signaling the start of another day.

"What's the range on that?" Michael asked, nodding towards the rifle.

"Not sure. The pellets will travel kinda far I think, but accuracy ain't worth a shit," Paul informed him. "They spread out the further they go."

"I see," Michael said as he looked out the window. "So, where's the other one you shot?"

"Oh, he's around somewhere. Hard to tell because they're all covered in blood."

"See that group over there?" Michael asked, pointing towards a group of a half dozen zombies staggering around the outskirts of the property.

"Yeah."

"Try for a headshot," Michael suggested.

"Which one?" Paul asked.

"One of the ones in the middle."

Paul aimed the rifle and squeezed the trigger. Michael was expecting the shot, but it still made him flinch. Three of the zombies went down, while two of them barely flinched from the impact of the pellets. One of the downed zombies stood back up.

"Two for one! Not bad," Michael said admiringly.

"So, what's that prove?" Paul asked, not sure where Michael was going with his little experiment.

"The pellets spread far enough that it hit five of them. Nice shooting by the way."

"Good shooting," Paul corrected him.

"What?"

"Good shooting. There's no such thing as nice shooting."

"That's kinda profound for you. No offense," Michael said with a smile.

"Heard it in a movie," Paul answered.

"Really? Which one?" Michael asked.

Paul looked at Michael and grinned, "Land of the Dead."

Michael blinked.

"Seriously? You're quoting lines from a zombie movie?"

Paul laughed.

"What can I say? I'm a huge Romero fan. Would you prefer I quote Shakespeare?"

Michael shook his head in amusement as Paul leaned out the window and yelled, "Oh, Romeo, Romeo, where for art thou, Romeo?"

"I see your point," Michael laughed. "You're a disturbed individual with a morbid sense of humor. You know that, right?"

"Yeah."

They both laughed.

"So," Paul reminded him, "the point to all this?"

"Oh, yeah. That was a pretty good distance away, and five of them got hit. You said earlier that the impact knocked one down, but then he got back up. I'm guessing it wasn't a head shot."

Paul nodded and Michael continued, "These zombies were farther away so the impact was minimal. The ones hit in the chest barely flinched, but the ones that were hit in the head still went down, and stayed down."

"Which proves what?" Paul asked.

"That it doesn't have to be a massive blow to the head to take them out. So maybe a baseball bat to the head will be just as effective as a gun."

"Just like in the movies," Paul smiled.

"Just like in the movies," Michael agreed, "So, if you were in a George Romero film and you were stuck in a secret, mountain laboratory surrounded by zombies, what would you do?"

Paul thought for a moment and smiled.

"Well," Paul answered, "first I'd bang all the girls, then I'd throw the nerdy science geek to the zombies to distract them while I made a run for it."

Paul laughed, but Michael did not.

"It was a joke," Paul explained.

"What?" Michael said as he stared absently out the window. "Yeah, I know."

"Oh, damn! There he goes again." Paul leaned the gun by the windowsill. "I'm heading downstairs to get a drink. Try not to shoot yourself."

Michael nodded.

"And watch out for those little, green men with purple afros," Paul added.

Michael nodded again.

"Yep," Paul said to himself as he turned to head back downstairs. "Mr. Cloak-and-Dagger is off to Never-Never Land again."

"Where's Michael?" Lauren asked as Paul entered the lab.

"Upstairs having wet dreams about George Romero."

"What?" Lucy asked.

"Nothing. He's working shit out. You know Mikey, once he goes deep in thought, you girls could walk by him naked and he wouldn't even notice."

"Wanna try?" Lauren laughed.

"If you do, I'm going with you," Paul laughed until Lucy punched him in the arm.

"I can't believe you guys would joke at a time like this."

"Lucy, relax," Paul suggested. "Now is the best time to let off a little steam or else we'll all go insane not knowing what's gonna happen next."

"What is going to happen next?' Emma asked in a frail voice.

Paul looked at her. She still looked like she would jump out of her skin at any moment.

"I don't know," Paul said. "But Mikey is working on something. If there's a way out of this mess, he'll figure it out."

"Be careful," Lucy said with a smile. "You almost sound like you're looking up to him."

"Now who's cracking jokes?" Paul laughed.

"I'm just gonna have to plaster it all over Facebook and Twitter that big bad Paul has grown fond of our little Mikey."

"Now, that's fucking funny," Paul laughed before Emma spoke in a voice barely louder than a whisper.

"Umm, guys," she said sheepishly. "Speaking of Facebook and Twitter, has anyone checked to see if any of those computers have internet access?"

They stared at her, speechless.

"I mean, this whole lab is run by computers, and we know there's no phone... so how did that doctor guy talk to people? There must be someone he needed to stay in contact with."

"Who needed to stay in contact?" Michael asked as he came around the corner.

They jumped to their feet and ran to a keyboard. Michael stared, confused as to what they were talking about, but none of them touched the keyboard.

"Robin, are you there?" Lucy asked.

"Yes, Lucy, I am here," Robin replied as her face appeared on the monitor.

"Do you have internet access?"

"Yes."

"Great!" Lucy said excitedly. "Emma you're a genius! All we have to do is go online and get help!"

"I'm afraid that is not possible," Robin informed her.

"Not possible?" Lucy asked. "Why not?"

"The internet signal we receive from the satellite is currently unavailable."

"Unavailable?" Paul asked. "How the hell can a satellite be unavailable?"

"There is a problem with the satellite receiver," Robin explained.

"Receiver? You mean the dish?" Lauren asked.

"That is correct."

"What's the problem?" Michael asked.

"I will show you," Robin announced as her face on the computer screen switched to the view of a large satellite dish in the middle of a grassy clearing. The dish lay on its side, a broken wire swayed lifelessly above it.

"What the hell happened to that?" Paul asked.

"There was a storm," Robin informed them. "The receiver was damaged."

"Well, why didn't you fix it?" He demanded.

"Sure Paul, "Robin replied, "I will walk outside and get right on that for you."

The gang said nothing, then Paul spoke up, "Did that fuckin' computer bitch just crack a joke?"

A smile appeared on their faces; it disappeared equally as fast.

"Can you fix it, Mikey?" Paul asked.

"You mean go out there? With those things?"

"Yeah, you're right, Mikey," Paul agreed, disheartened. "It's not like we are tricking a dumb-ass bear this time."

"But maybe we can trick them with smell," Michael said as he explained his initial idea. The hours crawled by as Michael and Paul discussed, and occasionally argued, about how to reconnect the broken wire. It pained them to admit that even if they somehow managed to distract those things long enough for Michael to fix and reattach the broken wire, the dish itself still had to be realigned. And that was a task that required brute strength; something Michael surely lacked, and Paul couldn't help him move the dish *and* watch Michael's back to fend off attackers.

The next problem was even worse: they didn't know how long those things would be distracted, or if they even could be. Eventually, they grudgingly agreed that fixing the dish was not a viable option.

The sleep-deprived girls had already slumped on the floor in the lab, though none of them actually slept. The only thing worse than the nightmares they saw when they closed their eyes were the nightmares they saw when they kept them open. Knowing those nightmares walked around outside meant no one was going to be able to get any real sleep.

Chapter 11 – Father

"Good evening, this is Clay Buffer with the Atlantic Television Networks 6 o'clock evening news." Clay hesitated, then yanked out his earpiece and flung it on his anchor's desk so he didn't have to listen to this producer repeatedly tell him to stick to what was written on the teleprompter.

"There's no other way to tell you this," Clay said, pain and fear evident in his voice; his composure all but lost. "So I'll just come out and say it. Our very own Jess Jessup has been struck down by what officials are now calling the Margaree Virus, or more simply, the M-Virus. The death of Jess has made it painfully clear that the M-Virus had in fact left the Margaree area and is rapidly spreading.

"Reports of virus-like activity are coming in from Glace Bay, Christmas Island, Whycocomaugh, Bell Cote, Neil's Harbor and Meat Cove."

"Joining us in the studio today, Clay announced as he turned to the gentlemen seated next to him, "is world-renowned biochemist, Doctor Bajeet Chopra. Doctor Chopra, could you please explain to our viewers," Clay hesitated again, his professionalism all but gone. "Well, in short, can you tell us what in the hell is going on?"

"Of course Mr. Buffer, and I thank you for having me. Upon examination of the viral fluid collected from the hosts and victims, it is apparent that a viral strain was introduced into the hosts' system, modifying the hosts' DNA into a new strand. There is no known organism that can biologically manufacture the DNA found in said viral fluid, so therefore it stands to reason that this new strand of virus DNA, although chemically complex, was manufactured."

"Excuse me, Dr. Chopra," Clay interrupted, "manufactured? Are you telling me that someone purposely made the M-Virus?"

"Yes, and no. The most important detail we are missing is the chemical structure of the original virus strand. We can only test the fluid from an infected host, or its victim, and not the original virus strand that created them. So although it is true that somebody has indeed created the M Virus, I strongly believe the M-Virus has mutated from its original purpose."

"And what was the original purpose?"

"We do not have enough data to determine what the original purpose of this rogue virus strand could have been. We do know that it is not airborne as the CDC originally reported, and we recently discovered that the M-Virus is in fact, waterborne. It is the most peculiar thing," Dr. Chopra said, almost admiringly, "instead of diluting in water, this particular strand of virus grows stronger. The longer the virus is in the water, the more it replicates itself. Once the host drinks the water, he or she immediately starts to undergo metabolic changes as the virus modifies the host's DNA, which, unfortunately, kills the host in a few hours. But as I mentioned, I do not believe this particular virus was designed to kill. If it was, then whoever created it is taking the long way around."

"The long way around? I'm confused."

"The M-virus does in fact kill the host, but strangely enough, the virus then revives the host's most basic bodily functions. It is only after this 'resurrection' so to speak, and I use that term very lightly, but it is after the host comes back to life that he or she shows signs of extreme violence and cannibalistic behavior."

"What you are describing Doctor Chopra sounds like. . . well, a zombie?"

"Not in the Hollywood sense of the word, but, yes, the host is more or less a zombie."

"How is that even possible?" Clay never looked into the cameras as he spoke, He was focusing all his attention on the doctor.

"If we speculate," Dr. Chopra explained, "we could assume that any virus capable of reanimating the dead will most likely have characteristics similar to the Ebola Zaire Virus. That particular strand effectively turns the human host into a mush of viral proteins that, in turn, feed upon healthy proteins. That particular virus does not affect the skeletal muscle or bones, and it is one of the few viruses known to man that are borderline parasitic. The DNA mutation of the M-Virus allows for Adenosine Triphosphate, or ATP."

"You've lost me, Doc"

"It is basic biology. The oxygen in our cells has a negative charge," Dr. Chopra's tone seemed to have switched from an expert in virology to that of a high school teacher. "Electrons want to be with protons, so the negative charges repel each other. Because the negatively charged cells are always trying to get away from each other, there is a lot of potential energy there. The ATP process can power needed reactions by losing one of its phosphorous groups to form ADP.

"Food energy, in this case, the oxidation of glucose, converts it back so that the energy is made available again. In other words, you use the energy from this process to do what you need to do to keep alive. It then recharges through the oxidation of glucose in a cycle called the TCA, or Krebs cycle, to provide energy for the conversion of ADP back to ATP."

The look on Clay's face told Dr. Chopra he needed to simplify his explanation.

"What all this basically means," Dr. Chopra continued, "is that the M-Virus uses the sugar in the host's blood and combines it with negatively charged oxygen cells, which creates life."

"But once the host dies, doesn't the glucose and negatively charged oxygen die with them?"

"You are very perceptive, Mr. Buffer. These zombie-like creatures indeed have no way of producing the basic building blocks of life, and this is where their cannibalistic nature comes into play. They need a constant supply of living blood cells for the conversion process to repeatedly go through the cycle.

"We do not know if it is by nature or by design, but by limiting the hosts to only being able to perform the most basic motor functions with practically no brain function, it drastically reduces the amount of energy used, thus allowing these zombie-like creatures to survive for a longer period of time between recharges."

"Recharges? You make it sound like we are nothing more than batteries."

"To the walking dead, that is exactly what we are: batteries."

"Well, folks," Clay announced as he finally turned his attention back to the camera. "You heard it here first - the undead walk the earth, and we are the new Duracell. Once again, that was Doctor Bajeet Chopra with his fascinating and somewhat disturbing explanation of what, and how, these zombies came to be. Thank you for joining us, Doctor Chopra"

"You're most welcome."

"Up next, the weather... Batteries. Amazing!"

Robin's computer screen flashed a series of camera views then stopped at the main door.

"Father?"

Robin's voice startled Lucy. Her tired eyes tried to focus on Robin's monitor. When she saw what was displayed there, she screamed.

"Robin! No!"

Lucy's scream drowned the rumbling of the steel security doors as they noisily opened.

"What's going on?" Michael said as he wiped the sleep from his eyes.

"Look!" Lucy yelled and she pointed to the monitor. Her hand trembled uncontrollably.

The screen showed a man wearing a lab coat walking through the open door. Before the mysterious man disappeared off screen, Michael noticed two things about him that sent a cold chill down his spine. The first thing was the man was covered in blood. The second thing he noticed scared him even more…

He looked dead.

"Oh, shit," Michael mumbled under his breath as Paul stood next to him and leaned down to get a closer look at the monitor.

"Robin, seal the lab," Paul ordered.

Robin ignored him.

"Robin, close the doors now and seal the lab!" Lucy demanded, but Robin did not react.

Robin's face finally appeared on the screen. With an innocent smile she announced: "Father's home."

Chapter 12 – The Attic

"Upstairs!" Paul yelled. Everyone scrambled for the door. Paul and Lucy stopped at the bottom of the stairs when they realized Emma was not with them. They turned to see Emma frozen with fear.

"Emma! Run!" Lucy yelled, but it was no use. Emma's eyes were fixed on Heslin, her feet paralyzed in fear. Heslin's putrid hands reached for her.

"Paul, do something!" Lucy pleaded. Paul's eyes widened in horror but he did not move to help her. Lucy moved to help her friend but Paul held her firmly.

"Do something! Emma! Run!" Lucy begged, but neither of them moved. Emma did not run; Paul did not help. He just tightened his grip on Lucy as she struggled to break free.

"It's too late," Paul yelled as he dragged Lucy up the steps.

"No! We can help her!" Lucy pleaded as Heslin pulled Emma towards him.

Emma screamed as Heslin's teeth sunk deep into her neck. Lucy screamed in horror as blood gurgled from Emma's throat when Heslin ripped a piece of flesh free. Lucy struggled helplessly in Paul's grip as Emma eyes met her's. Lucy struggled and screamed and cried and begged, but Paul refused to loosen his grip and continued to drag her up the stairs. Lucy watched helplessly as more of those zombie things appeared and started ripping into Emma's flesh. Lucy was crying and fighting to help her friend as Paul forced her up the stairs and out of view.

Emma's screams were deafening. When they suddenly stopped, Lucy's felt her knees weaken as another flood of tears raced from her eyes. Emma, the girl she considered to be one of her closest friends, was gone.

Paul tried the first door he saw but it was locked. Without hesitating, he threw his massive shoulder into it. The frame shattered helplessly. Chunks of splintered wood flew across the room like a rain of wooden darts. Lauren screamed and started to climb out of the window.

"Lauren, wait!" Lucy yelled. "It's us!"

Lauren paused on the windowsill, tears running wildly down her cheeks, then ran to Lucy.

"I saw," Lauren cried as she hugged Lucy tightly. "I saw what happened to Emma."

Paul looked out the window. Those creatures were still outside, but they were headed towards the house. He knew that soon they too would be inside and headed upstairs. He looked at the shattered door. A pang of remorse and regret flooded his thoughts as he remembered joking with Wade about locking the cabin door again. Paul pushed it aside and frantically scanned the room. Panicked, he looked up.

"Here!" Paul shouted, pointing to the ceiling. "We can get into the attic. They won't be able to climb up there."

He jumped and easily punched the hatch out of the way. He jumped again and slowly pulled himself up into the tiny opening in the ceiling, then reached his muscular arm down.

"Give me your hand, Lauren!" he ordered.

She reached up and he effortlessly pulled her up through the hole.

"Lucy, c'mon!" he yelled, but she didn't reach up. "Lucy, give me your hand!"

"Where's Michael?" she asked, looking back towards the broken door.

"Fuck Michael! Give me your hand," he barked at her. "C'mon, Lucy! Michael can take care of himself. Get your ass up here, now!"

The zombie-like people started to pile into the room as Lucy jumped for Paul's outstretched arm. One of them reached for her, its decomposing hand grabbing tightly around her ankle. Paul pulled harder, yanking the zombie off its feet and almost into the attic space with them. Its grip slipped and it crashed to the floor.

"Ok," Paul said, breathing heavily. "We're safe for now."

"We need to find Michael," Lucy told him, barely able to catch her breath.

"No problem," Paul huffed, "we need to be very careful up here. This attic is not much more than a crawl space, so we need to stay on the boards that run on top of the rafters. Got it?"

They nodded.

"If you go off the boards," Paul warned them, "you're going to fall through the ceiling."

"That's not good," Lauren said in a terrified voice.

"No," Paul said with a tiny smile. "That's not good. Lauren, you head towards that light over there. It's a vent to let the heat out."

Lucy wiped the sweat from her eyes. "It's not doing a very good job."

"Attics get hot," Paul stated matter-of-factly. "If we don't get some air in here, we'll dehydrate in a matter of minutes."

"What do you want me to do?" Lucy asked.

"Look for another vent," Paul suggested, "and kick it open. Do whatever you can to let air in."

"What are you going to do?" Lucy asked.

Paul wiped the sweat from his eyes and smiled. "I'm gonna find Mikey."

The girls slowly started crawling, Lauren towards the light, Lucy trying to find another vent in the opposite direction. Paul tried to follow the power lines in the dimly lit attic. He knew each octagon-shaped metal box was for an overhead light to one of the rooms below. When he got to the first box he punched a hole next to it. Sweat poured down his forehead and stung his eyes as he ripped at the lats and drywall, being careful not to lose his balance and fall through the ceiling.

"Mikey," he called, barely louder than a whisper as he moved his face closer to the hole he created. "If you can hear me, whistle."

He listened intently but heard nothing. He followed the wires to another junction box and punched another hole.

"Mikey, you there?"

Nothing.

"Arrgghh!"

Paul heard Lauren scream.

"Help me!" she screamed again.

Paul crawled along the beams as fast as he could go, sweat pouring down his face. As he rounded the huge, brick chimney, he saw Lauren's head and shoulders poking up through the floor, her arms flailing like someone who fell through thin ice.

"Shit!" he yelled.

"What is it?" He heard Lucy shout, but he couldn't see her in the dim light.

"She fell through!" Paul replied as he reached Lauren and started to pull her back up.

"Damn, you're heavy," he grunted as Lauren continued to scream and claw at him. "Stop squirming!" he ordered, but she wasn't listening. Her screams were deafening. "You're too heavy when you're squirming like that."

Paul pulled again but still couldn't lift her.

"Why is she so heavy?" Paul wondered.

"Fuck!" Paul yelled as realization set in.

As Lauren continued to scream, Paul held her tight and leaned over the hole to look at what was beyond her. Dozens of hands pulled on her. Others were biting. Lauren's once smooth and sexy legs were pitted with deep gashes and gushed blood. Paul's muscles bulged as he fought against the pull of zombies. The horrific sounds of chewing and screaming rang in his ears as he braced his feet against the rafters, closed his eyes, gritted his teeth, and pulled.

This time Lauren popped up through the hole with a wet slushy sound. She landed on his chest when he fell backwards.

"I got you!" he said as he exhaled deeply.

Lauren stared at him wide-eyed, but she didn't answer.

"You're ok now," Paul told her soothingly, "I got you."

Lauren's big brown eyes continued to stare at Paul, the look of horror still frozen on her face. Lucy screamed.

Paul turned to look at Lucy, her hand shaking violently as she pointed at Lauren. Paul looked past Lauren's unblinking eyes and over her shoulders. His gaze followed the curve of Lauren's back down to her supple waist, but that was where his gaze stopped; that was where Lauren stopped. Everything below her hips was gone. This time, Paul screamed.

Horrified, he flung Lauren's lifeless body away from him and scrambled towards the tiny slits of light created by the vent. He kicked the wooden vent. It shattered into splinters. Paul stuck his head into the tiny opening, inhaling the air and then threw up.

A hand on his shoulder sent a wash of fear over him. He spun around violently and instinctively pushed it away.

Lucy flew backwards across the attic from Paul's push and crashed through the floor.

One of her feet caught in the roof truss, preventing her from falling all the way through. As she swung like a human pendulum, her eyes could not focus on the zombies walking towards her as they swayed in and out of view.

Lucy screamed for Paul, but he didn't answer her.

Lucy tried a sit-up movement to grab the edges of the hole in the ceiling.

One of her hands grabbed the old plaster. It shattered in her grip, but her other hand gripped something solid. Her right arm and leg dangled helplessly just out of reach of the zombies, while her other hand and foot held her close to the ceiling.

"Paul, I'm stuck! Help me!"

Paul still did not answer.

Lucy could hear him kicking the vent. It sounded like he was tearing the house apart. She managed to pull herself up a bit more. Her arms shook under the strain. She grabbed again with her right hand, and this time got a secure hold. She was wedged between the rafters and trusses in such a way that she could not pull herself up any further. She had to keep her right leg pressed tightly against the ceiling, lest the zombies below would reach it and drag her down.

She had no intentions of letting that happen, but she also knew it would not take long for the strain of holding herself up against the ceiling would tear at her leg and stomach muscles and eat her strength.

She couldn't risk kicking her other foot free to try and pull herself completely out of the hole because that was the foot that kept her from falling. She was stuck between the proverbial rock and a hard place. Her grip and her strength were slowly failing her.

"Paul!" she yelled again.

Paul finally stopped and turned to face her.

"I'm slipping. Help me."

But Paul didn't move, he just stared as she struggled to keep herself from falling.

"I can't hold on much longer… Help me!"

Paul remained motionless.

"Get me the fuck out of here!" She yelled then started thrashing about, trying to pull herself into the attic.

Lucy stopped thrashing when she saw the look in Paul's eyes.

"Paul?" She asked, barely louder than a whisper.

Paul slowly turned his head towards the huge hole he'd kicked in the wall, then back towards her with emotionless eyes.

"Paul?" She repeated as panic grabbing her soul.

Lucy blinked a few times to see if her eyes were playing tricks on her. Her fingers were growing tired and she readjusted herself, trying to take the weight. Her mind swam dizzily in confusion. She looked down at the monsters reaching for her, then looked back to the hole in the wall where Paul stood just seconds ago.

As Lucy struggled to keep from falling, she kept mumbling the same three words: "He left me!"

Chapter 13 – What I Always Wanted To Do

Lucy could hear the zombies below but forced herself not to look. What she was heard frightened her. As if hanging for dear life above a group of flesh-eating zombies was not frightening enough, the sound of their grunts and groans made it worse. Then she heard what sounded like furniture being moved. Her heart pounded in her ears. If they learned to move furniture, they would be able to climb up and reach her.

She screamed and struggled against her twisted foot. She cried and screamed and begged and twisted and cried some more. That's when she felt it. The hands.

The hands reached up and gently touched her waist. So soft was the touch that she froze instantly. Her heart pounded so hard she thought it was going to explode. Yet, despite her panic, her muscles had failed her. They would not move; she was frozen with pure, unadulterated fear.

She clenched her eyes tightly in frightened anticipation as she felt something move closer to her head. She could feel its breath in her ear just seconds before she heard, "Shhhhh."

It took a moment for the sound to register; her brain was thoroughly busy watching her life flash before her clenched eyes.

"I got you," the voice said lovingly as those gentle hands pushed her upwards.

Her brain was still swimming in confusion, but she managed to wiggle herself free and pull herself completely into the attic. She looked back and saw those same hands grab firmly onto the rafters, and with a grunt, the head and shoulders came into view.

"Michael!" she gasped breathlessly as she threw her arms around him in a crushing hug. "I thought I was the only one left."

He tentatively put his arms around her to return the hug, and she buried her face in his chest and cried. He gently stroked her hair as she sobbed inaudible words. He looked around the attic space, noticing the daylight as it raced in from a giant hole in the wall and illuminated Lauren's lifeless torso.

Michael allowed himself to cry with Lucy.

Composing himself, he looked around again and asked, "Paul?"

Lucy finally raised her head. "He-he left me," she sobbed.

Michael's mouth moved, but she could not hear any sounds. Was he muttering some sort of curse, or was he simply left speechless? Loud banging from below startled them. Lucy let out a small scream.

"Come on," Michael said, leading her to the hole in the wall.

He stuck his head out and looked around, "This leads to a little roof a few feet below. It looks like you can jump to the ground from there. Just remember to roll when you hit the ground. The last thing you want to do is sprain an ankle. All of those things are inside the house right now, but I don't think they'll stay in here much longer."

Lucy nodded.

"Take this," Michael pulled the machete from his backpack and handed it to her. Lucy looked at the machete then to Michael, confused.

Michael passed her a bottle of water. "It's the only one I have, so don't drink it all at once."

"Michael?" Lucy started to say.

"Now listen," Michael said, gently holding her face in his hand, "keep on the road. They don't move very fast, so you don't have to keep running and tire yourself out. Just stay ahead of them. If some more come up the road, wait until the last minute, then duck into the woods…"

"Michael?" she repeated.

"Listen, this is important!" he said cutting her off. "Cut into the woods but keep close to the road. As soon as you get around them, go back on the road and run until you are far enough ahead of them. Do you understand?"

"Michael, I…"

"Do you understand?"

"No! No, I don't understand! Why you are telling me this?. Aren't you coming with me?"

"I can't."

"What do you mean you can't? I can't do this by myself. Michael, I need you to…"

"You can do this!" he ordered. "You have to do this!"

She started to cry. This time he didn't hug her, he just stared into her eyes and took a slow deliberate breath.

"Lucy, you have to get off this mountain and warn people."

"Come with me, Michael!" she pleaded

"I can't go with you, Lucy."

"Why not?"

Michael didn't say anything at first; then he held up his hand and pulled back his sleeve revealing a bite mark on his forearm.

"I--- I don't understand."

"Yes, you do." Michael forced a smile. "Have you ever watched a zombie movie?"

Lucy looked at him, confused.

"What happens when a zombie bites you?" Michael asked.

Lucy's eyes opened in horror.

"You don't know that!" she pleaded, but his index finger gently touched her lips. She stopped talking.

"We don't know that it won't," he explained, "and I can't be around you if it does."

Lucy looked outside, then back to Michael, tears freely running down her cheeks.

"What are you going to do, Michael?"

Michael looked around the attic and smiled, "I was thinking about maybe putting in a hot tub over there---"

Lucy punched him playfully in the arm. "That's not funny!" she said through her tear-filled eyes.

"I'm going to do the one thing I always wanted to do," he said, the smile gone from his lips.

"And what's that?" She sobbed.

"This."

Michael leaned towards her and kissed her gently on the lips. Lucy's eyes stared at him for the briefest of moments then slowly closed. She felt herself go limp in his arms and kissed him deeply.

No more words were said after that; there was nothing more to say. Lucy hugged Michael tightly in silent protest, but he pulled her arms away and without saying a word, begged her to leave so she could survive.

There are times in people's lives when words are not needed. If only people could communicate that well when their lives were not in danger.

They both knew what had to be done. She had to leave; he had to stay. They had already said their goodbyes.

Lucy climbed out of the hole, and Michael eased her down to the ledge below. Her tears were flowing again when she rolled on the ground and looked up to Michael. His eyes filled with tears as he watched the girl he always loved leave that God-forsaken place and run towards safety.

"Be safe my love," he whispered as she disappeared around a bend in the road.

Lucy ran from the lodge and down the steep road. She wanted to put some distance between her and the zombies. At least, that's what she was trying to tell herself. The truth was, she just kept going because she knew that if she stopped running away from the lodge, she just might turn around and run back to it, back to Michael.

She'd alternating between jogging and walking briskly for over ten minutes when she saw more of those zombie things coming up the road towards her. She tried to remember what Michael had said, but it was all a blur. The only thing she could remember was that kiss.

"Focus," she commanded her brain. "What did he say about the woods?"

Her mind raced back over the events. She still couldn't concentrate, and the new mob of zombies was getting closer. Not knowing what else to do, she turned and ran into the woods.

Night came much quicker in the trees. She was gasping for air. Her small feet pounded in the grassy forest bed, snapping tiny twigs as she ran deeper into the impossibly dark forest. The quick snapping of twigs below her feet contrasted with the slow, heavy thuds of the dozen zombie things that relentlessly pursued her.

Where was the road? If only she could find it. She needed to get out of the dense bushes and back onto the road. The laces of her running shoe snagged a low-lying branch and yanked her hard to the ground. Her panicked scream filled the brisk night air as she violently kicked at imaginary hands.

Her mind raced in fear as she kicked viciously at the empty air. It took her a moment to realize that nothing had grabbed her. She got to her feet, but a few steps later she felt the hard, damp ground punching her again. She felt around in the dark for the machete and her bottle of water. Grasping them tightly she climbed back to her feet, gulping in air. She was moving as fast as she could move in the dense brush, yet those things were gaining on her.

"They're not tripping in the dark," Lucy thought out loud.

She took a few more breaths to calm herself. Straying this far off the road was a bad idea; one that held the potential of being deadly. Taking another deep breath, she forced herself to walk so as not to keep tripping in the dark. She felt the damp, mossy floor under one of her left foot. Her dulled senses couldn't quite ascertain what that meant until she stepped on a sharp stick.

"Shit!"

At some point during one of her falls her shoe had come off. She quickly looked behind her but could see nothing. It was so dark. She could hear them getting closer.

"Fuck the shoe!" She said defiantly.

Prickly branches continued to slap at her bare, tender skin; others pulled at her hair. She tripped over a fallen log and landed heavily on a large rock. It slammed into her chest with a vengeance. She tried to shriek in agony, but no sound passed her lips. With the wind thoroughly knocked out of her, she protested in silence. Tears once again streaked her face. Panic engulfed her, followed by a feeling of complete helplessness. With no other response available from her exasperated brain, she curled into a fetal position and began to sob like a small child.

The eerie sound of rustling brush and snapping twigs grew dangerously close. She could hear their groans; she just didn't care anymore. Her lungs burned and her body shivered in the chilly night air. Her chest throbbed and her legs ached. She slowly and painfully rolled to her back on the cold, mossy carpet of the forest floor and stared up at a million tiny lights.

How pretty the stars looked.

How peaceful and serene.

Lucy screamed in horror as a putrefied hand reached down to grab her. Her mind snapped back into action and her body followed, refusing to die on this God-forsaken mountain! She screamed once more and kicked ferociously to escape the molesting hands. She scrambled to her feet and swung her giant knife. The sheathed blade bounced harmlessly off the zombie's head.

Lucy flung the sheath to the ground and swung the knife in a giant arc. The zombie creature never made a sound as its hands were severed at the wrists and fell to the ground, motionless.

Lucy snapped her leg forward, kicking the zombie. She swung the giant knife at its head. She missed the head, but the blade found its mark deep in the zombie's throat. Blackish-red blood oozed from the deep cut as she yanked the blade free. She grabbed the machete tightly with both hands and took a mighty, Babe Ruth swing just as the zombie moved forward and collapsed.

The blade missed the downed zombie, the force of her mighty swing flung her around like a child's spin toy. She crashed to the mountain floor, her eyes staring up at the multitude of stars once again.

"Get up!" She heard Michael's voice yell at her.

She sprung to her feet like a cat, her head jerking from side to side.

"Get moving!" She heard him say as clearly as if Michael was standing next to her like one of her coaches, barking orders like an army drill sergeant.

"I think I'm losing my mind," she said, realizing the voice was only in her head, but the voice of Michael ignored her, prompting her to get moving. Lucy heard bushes rustling just a few feet away. She didn't need voices to tell her to get her ass out of there. She hastened her pace, hoping, praying, that she could keep from tripping again when she felt something hard under her foot.

It took her a few more steps to fully comprehend that the soft, springy floor of the mossy mountainside had turned to a hard, flatter surface. She smiled triumphantly. She'd found the road.

With sunrise still a distance away, Lucy felt her way down the mountain road, her feet and hands warning her when she threatened to leave the dirt road. It was a long, slow battle staying on the road; the moonless night offered no help. Rocks were cutting into her foot, and it hurt like hell, but she limped forward.

She walked for hours trying to ignore the chilly air and the sharp rocks that occasionally dug into her shoeless foot.

She struggled forward, and morning finally broke.

Chapter 14 – The Van

Lucy quickly rummaged through the bags trying not to look at Wade's corpse. She found a bottle of water and took a long drink. It was disgustingly warm, almost hot, but it quenched her agonizing thirst. She poured some over her head as if trying to wash away the stench, then took another long, powerful gulp.

The water trickled down her face like tears, but she didn't have time to cry. She wanted to, she just didn't have time. She rifled through some more bags and found a pair of running shoes, socks, a t-shirt and more of the sun-roasted water. She grabbed her cache then stepped outside to escape the stench that burned her nostrils.

She lowered herself to the ground and gritted her teeth in pain as she peeled the blood-soaked sock from her beaten and battered foot. She took a deep breath and poured water over her wounds. Without taking the time to let the pain subside, she used one of the socks as a makeshift bandage to wrap her blistered foot.

She picked up her trusted machete, eased herself back to her feet. Her lightly-freckled nose crinkled as she gave the mob a defiant stare. Empty, emotionless eyes stared back at her.

The corner of Lucy's lip curled in disgust as she turned her back to them and started to jog.

Pain shot through her foot with a jolt and her thighs begged for mercy. She had only taken a few steps before slowing to a fast walk. She may have been an athlete, but all this running around in the dark and lack of sleep was taking its toll on her petite body.

That's when she heard it.

Her heart jumped in disbelief. It couldn't be. She listened intently. There it was again… a ringing sound.

"My cell phone!" Lucy cried out excitedly as she spun around to face the van. In her desperation to find water, her exhausted mind had completely forgotten that her cell phone sat waiting in the side pocket of her duffle bag.

And, it was ringing!

That meant there was a signal. That meant she could call for help! She was rescued! She took a few excited steps towards the van, ignoring her screaming foot, then froze in her tracks. Her heart sank.

Rescue was not within her grasp; something stood between her and being rescued. Something that instantly crushed her spirit.

Them.

They had already reached the van. Most of them just staggered past it and kept heading towards Lucy, but a few stragglers hung around the vehicle, attracted to the stench of death.

Lucy slowly walked backwards, her eyes darting side to side, taking in her surroundings as her exhausted mind raced through possibilities.

"Double-back through the woods," she thought excitedly. *"No, that won't work,"* she corrected herself, *"the zombies in the van might not leave, then I'll be surrounded."*

Her hand clenched the machete handle, turning her knuckles white.

"Kill the fuckers," She thought with a dangerous smile. *"Kill every last one of them."*

"There's too many," the other side of her brain warned her. A war raged inside her mind; her emotions and intellect battled for dominance.

Intellect won.

It was hopeless. Help may have only been a phone call away, but it was a call she was not going to be making. A loud crack jolted her mind back to the task at hand.

She looked from side to side for the source of the sound but saw nothing. She felt something tapping the top of her head. She looked up as tiny droplets of water kissed her face. The intensity increased abruptly. Moments later she was as wet as a trout.

She laughed sardonically. "Figures."

And, like so many times before, Lucy turned her back to the approaching mob and walked away, leaving her cell phone, and her last hope of rescue, behind.

Her laughter turned to sobs that shook her entire body. Tears flowed hot down her cheeks and melded with the cold rain. Her mind raced through recent memories, memories of her friends, of their happy, smiling faces. Those visions were replaced with the horror of watching death take her friends away from her. Faces screaming in agony as their young flesh was being ripped apart by monsters.

She hastened her pace as she limped forward in the chilling downpour, her determination resolute.

She was getting off this damn mountain...

Alive.

Chapter 15 - Crossroads

Lucy walked in a daze. She had no way of knowing exactly how long she had been walking, but she was fairly certain it had to have been at least two or three hours.

The rain had stopped almost as quickly as it had started, nothing more than a brief sun shower. Lucy thought God must be mocking her; the summer heat had returned in all its sweltering glory.

Her foot didn't hurt nearly as much, or perhaps it had just gone completely numb, Lucy wasn't quite sure but at least the pain had subsided a little.

"With my luck, I'll get gangrene and they'll have to amputate," Lucy said to the quiet trees that flanked the dirt road like birch and pine soldiers standing at attention.

The last thing she needed was to give her exasperated mind something else to worry about, but that new thought played on her mind and just wouldn't leave.

"I can see the headlines now… One-footed cheerleader walks down from the mountain, story at eleven."

"I must be going crazy," Lucy said out loud. "I'm cracking jokes about cutting my foot off. I wonder what time it is?"

Lucy was not the outdoors type who could tell the time by looking at the position of the sun. She was a cheerleader after all, not Davy Crockett.

"That's why people wear watches and carry cell phones," she thought, neither of which she had at the moment. Not that she ever carried a watch, no one did. Well, except for her grandparents, and her father on special occasions, like a wedding or funeral, or anything to do with going to church for that matter. Lucy was fairly certain that the only reason he wore the watch was because it would be rude to keep pulling out a cellphone during church services. A watch was a little more discreet.

"My cell phone," she said to the still quiet trees, but they didn't answer her. "I miss my pink Blackberry."

She knew if she had the damn thing she would know the time, she could even listen to some music to occupy her mind to avoid thinking about gangrene and amputating her foot.

"Or call for help," the logical part of her brain suggested.

"Help would be good," she answered. "Oh great, bad enough I'm talking to myself, now I'm answering myself too. I really am losing it."

Lucy glanced behind her.

"Yep, they're still there," she announced to the disquieting forest.

"Why hasn't anyone come for me?" she asked herself. "Didn't Mom and Dad wonder where in the hell I was when I didn't return home from the competition? Why didn't my over-protective father send out the entire Glace Bay Police Department and half the RCMP to find his daddy's little girl? Where in the hell is everybody?"

Those thoughts troubled her; she quickly pushed them out of her mind. She couldn't remember how long it had been since she walked past her cabin. She hadn't gone in, there was no point; there was nothing in there of value and, thanks to Wade, she couldn't even lock the door.

"Poor Wade," she thought as images of his shattered face crept back into her memory. "At least he didn't have to live through this horror."

When Lucy breached the top of a blind crest, the road ended at a stop sign.

The Seal Island Bridge was to the left, Cheticamp was to the right. She knew the bridge was closed, that's how she got in this damn mess in the first place. She also knew that if the cop wasn't still there, it meant a dead end. She could try to swim across the channel, but the current ran that ran in and out from the Atlantic Ocean was very strong, so that wasn't really much of a choice. She could be pulled under and swept out to sea. She quickly pushed that thought out of her mind as well.

"I didn't come this far," she said out loud, "to drown."

Cheticamp was more or less the same distance away, but there was no way of knowing if anyone was there either.

If Michael's theory was right and the problem started because something in that lab infected the water, then either direction should be protected by the mountains that surrounded Margaree.

"Water runs downhill, not up and over the next mountain," Lucy said thoughtfully. "So either direction has about the same chance of being safe."

She glanced over her shoulder again. Safe was such a relative term these days.

Kelly's Mountain and Hunter's Mountain would be hell to walk over, and Lucy was sick of mountains. The road to Cheticamp weaved through the valley and around the base of a mountain, then ran up along the coast.

"Cheticamp it is," she announced to no one as she turned right, but she didn't take a single step. A thought at the back of her mind caught her attention. Like a name stuck on the tip of your tongue but can't quite remember, she couldn't grab hold of that thought but something inside her told her that she needed to; it was important.

Lucy closed her eyes and tried to ignore the mob she knew would be upon her if she didn't start moving, but that thought was still lingering, wanting to be discovered.

"Distraction," she announced with a sly smile. She grabbed hold of the thought. She wasn't quite sure what she was supposed to do with it, but at least she recognized it.

"Back at the lab, Michael said something about distracting them with smell."

She looked again at the road behind her as the zombies approached the foot of the blind crest. The thought had morphed into an idea... a plan. Lucy smiled.

"Let's see if you fuckers are as dumb as you are ugly," she said coldly.

She pulled off her sneaker and peeled the blood-soaked sock bandage from her foot. The cuts had closed over and stopped bleeding. She stomped her bare foot on the pavement and winced in pain, then hobbled down the road to the left.

The road slapped and poked her tender foot without mercy as blood trickled, then poured, onto the hot pavement. She kept walking. More bloody footprints, more pain.

Lucy wiped some blood off her foot with the sock, balled it up and tossed it down the road. It did not go very far. She tore off a piece of her shirt, sopped up some more blood and then wrapped and tied it around a rock. She threw it but it didn't go very far either.

"Jimmy Fastball Williams you're not," she said with a small laugh as she tore another piece of her shirt, soaked up some more blood, and tied it around another rock.

She wound up like the baseball pitchers she'd watched on TV and let it fly. It passed her last attempt by only a few yards.

"Yep, you throw like a girl," she said, disgusted with her pathetic attempts and hoped it was enough. She looked towards the zombies to see if she had time to try again. They were getting too close. Lucy hoped Michael had been right about their sight too.

She quickly tore one more strip off her shirt, which now barely covered her breasts, wrapped her foot again, shoved it back into her shoe and ran to the right as fast as she could.

Her plan was simple: if the zombies took the bait and followed the scent, soon they would be walking away from her instead of constantly being on her ass.

When she thought she was far enough away she ducked into the trees to catch her breath and wait.

Time seemed to stand still.

Then she saw it, the first one… the big one that was always ahead of the others, leading them forward. She didn't think they were smart enough to have a leader. He probably just had longer legs so that put him in front of everyone else. He stopped at the crossroads.

Lucy held her breath. The anticipation was excruciating.

The zombies started to walk to the left. She almost squealed in excitement but muffled it back out of fear that they would hear her. It worked! All she had to do was wait for them to be out of sight and then run like hell. It was the perfect plan.

"Thank you, Michael," she whispered with a smile.

Her thoughts drifted back to Michael, how he had managed to stay calm throughout this crisis and figure things out, formulate plans… sacrifice himself.

She felt a tiny tear trickle down her cheek.

Her friends were gone. All of them. Well, almost all of them. She didn't know if Paul had made it off the mountain alive, but he was strong, so he probably made it even though the selfish son of a bitch left her to die… but the rest of them were dead.

Lucy allowed herself this brief moment of rest to feel sad; to hurt for the loss of her friends. After everything she'd been through, she deserved a few minutes to mourn her friends.

The smell hit her nostrils a fraction too late as a putrid hand grabbed her shoulder.

With a scream her instincts kicked in. In a move that would have made her cheerleading coach proud, she leapt into the air in a ballet-like spin and broke free from the monster's grip while adding a tremendous amount of torque to her knife hand; the machete's long blade sliced into the zombie's gaping mouth.

The blade easily severed the decomposing skull and bit into the tree behind it. As the body fell limp and crashed to the ground, the top half of the head remained perched on the machete blade. The sunken, dead eyes looked at Lucy, the light finally distinguished. They almost seemed apologetic. Seconds later the top half of its head succumbed to gravity and fell to the hard ground with a sickening thud.

Lucy struggled to remove the blade from the tree as she scanned for others; there were always others.

When the tree released its grip on the knife, she bolted towards the road to Cheticamp and froze in her tracks. She stared in disbelief. She released the breath she didn't know she was holding; a barely audible name slipped past her lips.

"Paul?"

She stared incredulously. It was Paul… but it was not her Paul.

Not the Paul she fell in love with when they were seniors in high school. Not the Paul who gave up a football scholarship to play for Notre Dame in favor of going to Cape Breton University because that's where Lucy was going to college. It wasn't even the Paul who had abandoned her and left her to die.

This Paul was dead.

"It's not really him anymore," Lucy tried to tell herself as he drew closer.

She raised the machete for the mighty blow that would finally end Paul's existence, the blade dripping with the blackish-red blood from the decapitation just moments ago. She stood taut like a cat ready to strike its prey, prey that was walking straight towards her.

Her determination faltered; the blade began to shake.

"Stop being squeamish," she commanded herself. "It's not Paul anymore. Just cut its damn head off and get out of here."

Every fiber of her being told her not to hesitate, but she couldn't help herself. It was still her Paul.

Lucy quickly looked behind her; her decoy had stopped working. Had they heard her? Had they heard that other zombie moan right before she cut off its head? Was Paul telling them she is here?

She didn't have any answers, only questions. The one thing she knew for certain was they were heading her way, and she was trapped between them and...

She looked back at Paul.

"I can't do this!" She cried out in desperation. "Please, God, help me!"

She looked behind her again. There were so many of them. She looked back to Paul, his massive frame now only a few feet away. She felt helpless. Her once athletic legs had failed her; she felt frozen in place, unable to move.

"Paul, don't!" she pleaded.

Paul grabbed her by the arms, pulling her closer.

"Paul, no. Please, I'm begging you. Don't."

Tears raced down Lucy's cheeks. Paul lowered his head towards her, mouth opened.

"Paul---" she said one final time, then pushed the machete upwards into his lower jaw until the hard steel sank deep into his skull.

Blackish-red blood ran down the blade and over Lucy's shaking hands. Paul dropped to his knees, his cold eyes still gazing longingly at her. She lovingly brushed his hair as a fresh wave of tears streaked her face.

"I'm sorry," she whispered, then wrenched the blade free.

Paul toppled sideways like a mighty oak and crashed onto the hard pavement.

Lucy took a deep breath, stepped over his bulking frame, and started walking towards Cheticamp without looking back.

Chapter 16 – Defeated

Lucy limped down the road, her pace slowing with each passing hour. Hunger was another pain she had to endure.

Images of her friends haunted her thoughts. Her determination all but vanquished, she released the last possibility of hope and fell to her knees, shaking like a thunder-frightened dog. She found her tears again.

"I'm not going to make it," she whimpered.

Her skin, slick with sweat in the hot sun, smelled of body odor and panic. She brushed her matted hair from her eyes and painfully rose to her feet. She stared at the empty road ahead of her, then slowly turned to face her pursuers.

Defeated, she raised her left arm towards them, palm facing up. With her right hand, she raised the machete above her shaking wrist.

"Fuck you," she said in a final act of defiance, then slowly lowered the blade to drag it across her wrist.

The hard steel gently kissed her soft skin as it creased around the edge of the blade in anticipation. Lucy closed her eyes to say a silent prayer before feeding the hungry blade.

"I'm sorry Mom," she whispered repentantly. "I'm sorry Daddy. I can't go on. I can't do this any mor---"

A thudding sound interrupted her final goodbyes. Lucy froze; the blade hungrily waiting for its reward. She turned to look for the source of the noise, but she couldn't see anything. The road twisted out of view ahead of her, behind her the groans of the hungry mob grew louder.

Then she heard it was again.

"*I know that sound,*" she thought. Her mind struggled to focus, attempting to identify the sound. The mob drew nearer, arms outstretched to take her.

"It's a door!" She yelled at them, then turned and ran.

The pain was gone. It still shot through her body like a bullet, but she couldn't feel it. Filled with adrenal and new hope, she ran until she rounded the bend in the road then stopped dead.

New tears ran down her face. There, in the midst of the thick, green spruce and tall white birch trees sat a tiny roadside café.

It was painted an ugly, faded yellow with ghastly blue trim, but that hideous looking restaurant was the most beautiful thing Lucy had ever seen.

She bolted towards it as fast as her exhausted legs could carry her.

Inside the café, a chubby waitress with swollen ankles smiled as she poured coffee into a big man's cup.

"Anything else I can get for ya Honey?" She asked.

"That's all, Rosie," he answered, watching his cup fill. "Thanks. Hey Rosie, when ya gonna to play some different music? Every time I stop here it's the same damn songs playing over and over again."

"And every time I give you the same answer Hank," she answered with a wink. "I already told you too many times to count, other radio signals don't get past the mountains. The only station we can get is the local French station. Parlez-vouz Francais?"

"Par-lay What?"

"Exactly. So we play cassette tapes so you truckers can at least understand the words to the---"

Rosie stopped midsentence when the sound of the screen door grunted against its hinges then slapped shut. Hank noticed how quickly Rosie lost her dimpled smile.

"Rosie? What's wrong?" Hank asked.

She didn't answer.

Rosie stood frozen in place as the coffee she was pouring spilled over Hank's cup. A deafening silence followed; forks and knives were not clinking on plates, diners were not chatting. Confused, Hank slowly turned on his squeaky stool to look at whatever had grabbed Rosie's attention. Everyone in the restaurant was staring towards the door. Hank followed their stunned stares.

There, in the doorway, stood a young girl who looked to be in her early twenties, holding a giant, blood-streaked machete. Her shirt was half ripped off her, her tanned legs covered in scratches too numerous to count, and she was covered in blood.

Lucy blinked slowly, trying to decide if the scene before her was real or some type of a mirage. Overwhelmed with exhaustion and relief, Lucy collapsed to the floor.

Everyone rushed to help her. Everyone except Hank…

His eyes were fixated on what he saw on the other side of the screen door.

###

Lucy's eyes fluttered open, and she found herself staring at a water-stained ceiling. A long, fluorescent bulb flickered. She could hear screaming and crying.

Her eyes tried to focus. She turned her head to the side to see a woman lying on the floor next to her, a look of horror frozen on her lifeless face.

"Is that blood?" Lucy wondered.

She turned her head to look in the other direction. Bright sunlight hurt her eyes as it poured in through a giant window. A shadow moved in front of the light, blocking her view. She couldn't make out any details of who stood in front of her like a giant eclipse. She took a slow, deliberate breath. Something burned her nostrils. It was that smell…

She knew that smell.

The eclipse leaned down towards her; the familiar smell of death and decay grew stronger.

Like a familiar old rerun, Lucy knew what was going to happen next.

Defeated, she closed her eyes and welcomed it.

Chapter 17 – The Mystery

Lucy's eyes fluttered open. Harsh bursts of light blinded her. She squeezed her eyes tight again to protect them from the burning light. The sudden intrusion of light lingered as tiny colored specks floated behind her lids, then slowly faded away. Lucy carefully opened her eyes again, using her hand as a shield. The slits of light slowly took form. The bright sunlight was held at bay with crisscrossing boards.

"The window is boarded shut," Lucy's groggy mind told her.

She closed her eyes until the floating specks of colored lights dissipated again, then refocused on the slits of bright light. The window was boarded up. Her mind raced for an explanation. It was only two heartbeats before her mind found an explanation and grabbed hold. The explanation raced through her entire body in the form of panic. She bolted straight up. The sudden movement made her head spin, or maybe the room was spinning. She wasn't sure.

She grabbed the blankets to steady herself and looked around the room. The door was also boarded up. It was comforting to know that nothing could get in, but that tiny level of comfort quickly faded with another realization… she couldn't get out either.

"Am I a prisoner here?" Lucy asked the empty room, her mind still racing. "Where is here?"

Lucy continued to look around the room. Hanging limply above the door frame was a smashed video camera. Images of the laboratory and Robin raced through her exhausted mind.

"How the hell did I get back here?" Lucy mumbled, realizing her lips were parched.

Next to the bed on a small table she saw a bottle of water, a drinking glass, and a videotape.

"What the…?" Lucy said as she leaned over to reach for the videotape.

Dizziness grabbed her again, and she fell to the floor with a loud thud. She lay on the floor, trying to collect her thoughts as she stared up at the ceiling.

A huge hole was punched through the ceiling a couple of feet from the light fixture. More horrifying images flashed through her mind. Piece by piece the puzzle was coming together. As she lay there putting the pieces together, her mind got stuck: a big piece of the puzzle missing.

She remembered, painfully, the events that led up to her leaving the lodge and finding the little café where she was certain she was about to die, yet here she was, back at the lodge.

"Did I dream the whole thing?" She asked the empty room.

It didn't give her any more clues. She pulled herself up to a sitting position and grabbed the water. She ignored the glass and put the bottle to her lips and drank. Her immediate thirst quenched, she noticed the videotape again. On the face of it was written in black marker: Play Me.

Lucy looked around the room and noticed a tiny camcorder sitting just below the window plugged into the power outlet.

"It must be recharging," she thought as she gently rose to her feet.

Her legs still a bit unsteady, she staggered towards the camcorder. Lucy succeeded in walking well enough to keep from falling over, but bending down to pick up the camera proved to be another matter entirely. Her already aching head bumped hard into the boards that covered the window when she leaned over to pick up the camcorder. She fell to her knees as another dizzy spell buzzed in her head. She fell back to the floor, once again staring up at the ceiling.

Lucy took a few deep breathes to calm her nerves then, with camera in hand, she carefully crawled across the floor. Crawling on all fours meant a shorter trip to the floor if she lost her balance again. It wasn't until she climbed back into the bed that she realized she wasn't wearing her own clothes. She was dressed, but they were not her clothes. She wore an old, button-down sweater that looked like something her grandfather would wear.

She slid her fingers between the buttons and felt her bare breast. She reached for her shorts and discovered they were also missing, replaced by a baggy pair of pants.

"Who did this?" Lucy thought, her heart racing.

Lucy rolled up a sleeve to reveal plenty of scratches, but no blood. She pulled up the pant leg. More scratches, but again, no blood. Uneasiness washed over her with the realization that someone had removed her clothes and bathe her while she was unconscious.

Another fear raced through her mind as she imagined herself lying naked while somebody bathed her. A tear escaped her frightened eyes as her heart pounded in her ears.

Lucy looked at the tape, wondering what it was she was supposed to watch and, more importantly, who made the tape?

Her mind raced through recent memories of what she did know. She remembered walking for what seemed like days to escape this place and now it appears she was right back where she started, bathed and wearing somebody else's clothes, with no idea who was responsible. She apprehensively flipped the tape in her hand as her eyes continued to scan the room.

Her thoughts were getting clearer now, though she still couldn't tell the nightmares apart; it all seemed so surreal. The nightmares that haunted her dreams overlapped the nightmares she was positive she had witnessed with her own eyes; yet it all seemed like one, bad dream. She was not sure which of the nightmares that haunted her mind really had happened.

As Lucy looked around the unknown yet strangely familiar room, her eyes stopped at the foot of the bed.

"What an odd place for a dresser," she thought, looking it over before settling her gaze on the hole in the ceiling above it. *"It wasn't put there as a dresser. It was being used as a ladder."*

Still thumbing the tape, Lucy continued to investigate the room. She tossed the tape on the bed and pushed herself back to her feet. The tiny table next to the bed held no other secrets, but at the far end of the room was a closed door. It was nailed shut like the other door.

"A closet?" She thought.

Lucy slowly inched towards the door, her hand hung suspended, inches above the doorknob.

Grownups smile knowingly when young children say there are monsters in the closet because they know there is no such thing as monsters. It hadn't been all that long ago when Lucy believed they weren't real too, but since then she learned that monsters were in fact, very real. Not the giant Godzilla-like creatures or aliens from space like you see in the movies; these monsters were different... they were us, except that they were dead and walking around eating people.

Who knew what monster was just beyond that door?

Lucy failed to keep her hand from trembling. It ached for her machete, but it was nowhere to be found. She looked at the other door boarded securely, then back to the closet door.

"No boards, no danger," she thought. She hoped.

Lucy lowered her hand and grasped the door handle. The squeaking sound of the turning handle filled the tiny room then Lucy heard the gentle click of the door latch being released. Gathering her courage, she quickly pulled the door open and ran back to the bed like a frightened child. She dove on the bed with such effort that she slid off it and crashed hard onto the floor.

"Fuck!" Lucy yelled as she pulled her elbow towards her in pain. She quickly looked under the bed towards the now opened closet. Monsters had not chased her out. She sat up and peeked over the bed. Still no monsters. So far so good.

Lucy stood up, her eyes never leaving the door, then cautiously walked back to the closet. Her heart pounded so hard she could feel her blood pulsating through her veins.

She darted her head in and out of the closet so fast it was as if she hardly moved at all, but it was enough for her to see that the closet was empty except for a row of clothes hung neatly on hangers. Mustering up more of her failing courage she took a deep breath and pulled the rack of clothes apart. She exhaled sharply in relief. It seemed silly once she'd done it, but she had to check that monsters were not hiding behind the clothes.

The closet held more clothes similar to what she wore: nondescript sweaters that smelled as if they had been hanging there a long time. She pulled her sweater to her nose. It had the same musty, unused smell.

On the floor of the closet she noticed a bucket and an old pair of shoes. She looked at her own feet. They were bare of course, but her cut foot looked like it had been cleaned and dressed by a doctor.

Lucy walked back to the bed, eyed the tape, and picked it up again. She knew she was supposed to play it, but she didn't know what she would see… or if she wanted to see it. None of this was making any sense, and she wanted to get as many answers as she could before watching the mysterious tape.

Lucy walked over to the window and looked through the slits at the world outside.

"Well, at least there are no zombies," she said with a smile, then remembered that the door was nailed shut from the inside. Her smile faded.

"Yet," she added with a sigh.

Lucy rifled through the drawers in the dresser at the foot of the bed. Folded boxers and tartan socks told her it was a man's room, an older man at that, but who or where he was she didn't know.

She shivered with the thought of an old man undressing her and putting her in his clothes and doing God knows what else while she lay unconscious on the bed. Staring aimlessly at the top of the dresser her eyes slowly focused on the dust. It took a few heartbeats for her weary brain to catch up. In the dust she could make out scattered footprints. Somebody had used it as a ladder to climb out.

"Well, obviously," she said to herself. "The door and window are nailed from the inside. How else are they going to get out?"

It was then that she noticed that some of the dust made a perfectly straight line, and a little behind that, another shorter line.

"That kinda looks like something a picture frame would make," she thought.

"But where's the picture?" She said out loud.

She looked around the room again and noticed a small waste-paper basket in the corner that held a picture frame. As she picked it up, the tinkling of glass told her why the picture was thrown in the garbage; the smiling faces in the picture told her the who.

"Robin and her father," Lucy said to the empty walls. She looked up at the busted video camera. "This must be his room. So he and the Robin computer could talk to each other."

Lucy loved reading mystery novels and usually figured out 'who dunnit' long before the book ended. Occasionally, a book like Claude Bouchard's debut novel, *Vigilante,* managed to stump her, but usually, she solved the mystery. This mystery still had her stumped, and each clue she uncovered just added more questions.

Lucy started to tick off on her fingers what she knew so far to help her solve this mystery...

She was back in the lab on top of the mountain, there was no doubting that. Whoever changed her clothes, cleaned and dressed her foot knew what they were doing. That person was also fully aware of the danger and had secured the room to keep her safe. The mystery person had also left an escape route, which meant they were not keeping her prisoner.

Lucy knew it could not be Heslin because, well, he was dead. If by some miracle it was a different doctor that Robin had let in the house, then it still couldn't be Robin's father because he would have thrown out the broken frame but he would have kept the picture. Tears threatened to explode from her eyes as she remembered what Heslin had done to Emma. She pushed the vision aside, forcing herself to concentrate. She had watched all her friends die. Well almost all of them.

"Michael got bitten, so he is probably dead too," she thought, still fighting back the tears. *"So that leaves... no one."*

Lucy was back to square one. But another thought squeezed itself into her mind: Michael had been bitten, she'd seen the wound, but then realized this wasn't the movies, and these were not real zombies. Sure, they were dead and ate people, and…okay, they were zombies, but there was no proof that getting bit turned you into one. So maybe… just maybe…

"It's Michael!" she said triumphantly, not realizing how much she was smiling as she hastily slid the tape into the camcorder.

"Michael!" she repeated when she pressed play and his face appeared on the tiny camcorder screen.

As Michael explained how he figured she would head to Cheticamp instead of going over Kelly's Mountain where they knew the bridge was closed, and how he eventually found the café and managed to fight off the zombie seconds before it bit her, Michael started doing the strangest thing…

He started writing on a piece of paper. His talking never ceased but he wasn't making any sense and was saying mostly gibberish, then he held the paper up to the camera. Lucy held the tiny screen of the camcorder closer and squinted to read it more clearly.

Say nothing. Remember the cellar.

Lucy looked quizzically at the screen as Michael talked about irrelevant things like trees, mountains, birds and crickets. Her mind raced back to the cellar where she and Michael had discovered the room behind the steel door.

"This is not making any sense," she thought to herself as Michael wrote another message and held it to the screen.

I don't trust her.

"Trust who?" Lucy thought.

Once again her mind raced back to the cellar but she couldn't remember anything that would give her the slightest clue as to what Michael was talking about. Michael was reciting song lyrics now.

"What are you going on about?" She whispered in her mind.

His cloak and dagger nonsense was starting to get on her nerves, and that's when her mind grabbed hold - *cloak and dagger.* Michael was purposely trying to be confusing with what he was saying. But why?

Several realizations rushed to her at once: Michael had videotaped his message on a camcorder outside, where it was dangerous and not within the protective walls of the steel lab. Why would he risk doing it that way? Robin could have easily videotaped a message for him; this whole building was like a giant video camera.

Lucy looked above the door frame at the shattered camera. Robin might be able to still hear, but she could not see inside the room; she might be able to hear Michael's videotaped recording but she couldn't see the messages Michael wrote.

That's why Michael was quoting song lyrics and saying other nonsense... he was stalling, allowing Lucy time to figure it out.

Her mind raced back to the cellar and the conversation they had when a question Michael had asked her jumped back into her memory.

Can computers lie?

"This one can!" Lucy repeated the answer soundlessly.

It was then that Lucy realized the effort Michael had gone through to protect her in this room instead of just getting Robin to seal Lucy in the heavily secured lab... Michael did not trust

Robin. That meant Robin was up to something. Michael knew it, and he was…

"Gone," she whispered.

Michael had left her here. Her eyes started to tear as she looked at the tiny screen. Michael held up another message:

Looking for food. Stay in the room.

She watched Michael lean forward to shut the camera off, but then he paused.

He stepped back and softly whispered, "I can't wait to see you in that hot tub."

The screen went black, but Lucy had already left the camcorder on the bed and was climbing onto the dresser. At five feet tall she could just barely get her head into the attic. She pivoted cautiously on her perch as she looked around the dimly lit space. She could see the giant hole in the wall that Paul had kicked in, but she could not see Lauren's body.

"Michael must have moved her," she thought. And with that thought came another: *"Where did he put her? Where are the bodies?"*

Lucy climbed back down and sat on the soft bed. She rewound the tape and played it again. A few more drinks of water and Lucy suddenly realized her little bedroom fortress did not have a bathroom. Then she remembered the closet. She went back to the closet, looked at the floor and saw the bucket. Next to it on the floor was a roll of toilet paper.

"Water closet," Lucy laughed. "Mikey, you have a sick sense of humor."

Chapter 18 – Michael

Lucy woke with a start; she thought she heard something moving. She tilted her head and concentrated when she heard another clunking sound. She scurried to the dresser and started to jump into the attic. As she did, something hard cracked into her head, knocking her backwards. She fell on the bed and bounced sideways but managed to stop herself from tumbling to the floor.

She stared at the hole in the ceiling. She watched the outline of a head appear. A few seconds later, the head had somehow flipped, almost acrobatically, and the torso of a man was standing on the dresser, his head still in the rafters. The figure bent its knees permitting the owner to finally look at her, and her at him. Lucy exhaled sharply.

"Michael!" She said excitedly.

"Hi-ya, Luce," Michael smiled. "Going somewhere?"

"I heard a noise."

"Umm, yeah, that was me, sorry. It's not easy scaling up the side of a building. You didn't answer when I yelled so I figured you were still asleep." Michael rubbed his chin, "I think you dislocated my jaw."

"Sorry," she apologized as she bounced to her feet and hugged him. It was a long hug. If somehow had told her just a few days ago that hugging Michael would be one of the best feelings in the world, she would have laughed at the absurdity. But here, now, she didn't want to let go. His arms comforted her more than she thought possible. A thought raced in her mind and she suddenly felt uncomfortable. She released her grip and took a step back.

"Michael?" She asked.

"Yeah?"

"Did you enjoy the view?"

"What?"

Lucy pulled the wooly fabric of the sweater. "The view, did you enjoy it?"

"Oh, that," he said, his face reddening.

"And did you bathe me as well?" Her eyes burning with anger.

Michael lowered his head without saying a word. He didn't have to. Lucy punched him in the arm.

"I can't believe you'd stoop so low as to undress me when I was unconscious! How dare you? Of all the---"

"What the hell did you want me to do?" Michael said, cutting her off. "Leave you the way you were?"

"Yes!" she snapped back.

"Ok, fine," Michael said as he stepped off the bed, walked towards the window then spun to face her, his temper building. "The next time you're covered in blood and filth from zombies, I'll leave you like that!"

Lucy glared at him, arms on her hips.

"That way," Michael continued, "when you're sleeping you can rub your hands in that infected filth and possibly put them in your mouth!"

Lucy's icy stare broke.

Michael walked back to her and offered his hand to help her step off the bed.

"Lucy," he continued in a softer, caring voice, "I only did what I had to do to protect you. I'm sorry if I offended you."

"No, I'm sorry." She said. This time her face was reddening. "You're right Michael. I'm just being… silly."

"No," he answered, "you're just being Lucy."

She looked at him incredulously with her hands on her hips.

"And what's that supposed to mean?"

"You like it when guys look at you," Michael answered, "but only as long as you're in control."

That stung her more than a slap in the face. But, as usual, Michael was right. She'd lost track of how many times she flaunted herself in front of boys, and men, to get what she wanted. She enjoyed the attention and used it to her advantage.

"And, Lucy," Michael added with a sly smile, "the answer is yes… I did enjoy the view."

She punched him in the arm again, more playfully, but hard enough that he felt it.

"I'm so glad you're back," she said hugging him again. "I was so scared. I thought you left me."

"I would never leave you," he promised.

Michael could feel the warmth and softness of her body press into him. He closed his eyes tightly and started calculating complicated math problems in his head as a distraction before Lucy felt just how much he enjoyed having her pressed up against him. Another minute passed before she unlocked her arms from around him.

"Hey, I found some food," he said as he slipped off his backpack and lowered it to the floor.

Bottled water, a few bags of chips, a jar of peanut butter, bread, a bag of cookies and other junk food spilled onto the bed.

"A gourmet meal," Lucy laughed.

"It's hard to find anything that hasn't been tainted with water or needs to be cooked in water."

She picked up the bread.

"That might be a little stale," he explained, "But it was made before all this zombie stuff happened, so it should be safe."

Lucy checked the packaging date on the other items. Everything had been packaged at least two days or more before their whole world had collapsed.

"Michael thought of everything," she mused to herself, then picked up the jar of peanut butter. *"Well, almost everything."*

"Knife?" She asked.

Michael reached behind him and gripped the machete then stopped.

"I don't think either one of us wants to make a sandwich with that knife." He said, sliding it back into its sheath.

Lucy smiled and unscrewed the lid. She dipped her fingers into the jar then spread some peanut butter across the bread.

"Our fingers were good enough when we were kids," she laughed.

Michael reached for the jar, but Lucy pulled it away.

"Excuse me, I don't know where your fingers have been," Lucy said. Her face instantly flushed red.

"Not there!" His sharp reply told Lucy that he meant it.

"Lucy," Michael said as he leaned in closer. He could feel her warm breath on his face. "I would never do that to you," he whispered, their eyes locking.

"I know," she responded in a breathy voice, barely louder than a whisper. "But Michael, there's something I need to know."

"What's that?" He asked.

She pulled at the sweater. "Is this the best shirt you could find?"

They both laughed.

"It was in the closet," he grinned.

"It's a ratty old sweater, and it's a million degrees in here!"

"It's cooler at night, and with the windows boarded up, it takes longer to heat up," Michael explained.

"Oh."

Michael stuck his fingers in the jar and pulled out a dollop of peanut butter to slap on his bread. As he did so, he noticed the buttons on Lucy's sweater were spaced rather far apart, revealing a lot of flesh.

"I think the sweater looks nice on you," he told her. He could feel his face turning red.

Lucy looked down and noticed the large gap between the buttons.

"Ugh," she said pulling her sweater closed with one hand and pushing him with the other. "Men! Can you please find me something else to wear besides this? Its musty smelling. And I don't want to be playing peek-a-boo with you every time I move."

"I was beginning to like peek-a-boo," Michael laughed, still flushed with embarrassment as Lucy playfully pushed him. "But I will find something else for you later."

"Thank you," she said dryly. "And, Michael?"

"Yeah, Luce?"

"I'm sorry I got mad at you. You know…before."

"That's ok, Lucy, I understand. I would have done the same thing."

"Oh, please," Lucy laughed. "If you woke up and discovered that I stripped you naked and bathed you, you would be dancing with joy."

"No, I wouldn't. I would be pissed off."

Lucy didn't know how to take his response. His face told her he was being truthful.

"Why?" she asked.

"Because I would have been unconscious and missed it." Michael laughed as she punched his arm again.

They ate in silence after that. Lucy glanced at him a few times and occasionally caught him stealing a look between the buttons.

"Oh, for God's sake!" she said, standing up.

"What? What is it?" Michael asked.

Lucy stood in front of him, unbuttoned the sweater and let it fall to the floor. "Just look already. You're trying to peek at them without getting caught, and you're driving me up the wall! So just take a good look and get it over with!"

She held her hands on her hips defiantly and stared off in the distance looking at nothing. When she finally looked down, Michael was reaching for her sweater. As he stood, he gently pulled the sweater up over her shoulders and closed it in front of her.

"Lucy," he said in a soft soothing voice, "you are beautiful, sexy, and the most wonderful person I have ever known. I'm sorry if I offended you."

"Michael," she started to protest but he silenced her with a gentle finger to her lips.

"Lucy, I could spend hours getting lost just looking in your eyes, watching how your nose crinkles when you concentrate, or how your tongue darts out just a little to wet your lips before you speak. I could fill an entire day just watching how your hair brushes against your cheek. I'm sorry I was staring where I shouldn't have been looking, but you do not need to take your clothes off for me to enjoy the view."

"So you don't want to see me naked?" She blurted out, and instantly recognized how cold it sounded.

Michael just smiled his warm smile.

"What I meant was..." she tried to explain, but he silenced her again with a finger to her lips.

"The view," he smiled warmly, "is as magnificent as you are."

Michael leaned towards her. She tilted her head to receive him, but much to her surprise he didn't try to kiss her. Instead, he leaned into her ear and whispered, "I am sorry. It won't happen again."

"Liar," she smiled. Michael smiled with her.

"Would you believe I will try my best not to get caught looking?"

"That's better," Lucy laughed as turned her back to him to properly put the sweater on and button it. She sat back down on the floor facing Michael.

They laughed at each other as they stuck their fingers in the jar and tried to use them like a knife to spread the peanut butter on the bread. While they talked, Lucy noticed his gaze would still occasionally fell to her chest. She also noticed that it no longer upset her.

"You have some peanut butter on the side of your face," she told him. He went to wipe it away then realized his fingers were full of peanut butter.

Much to his surprise, and hers, Lucy leaned towards him licked it from his cheek.

Chapter 19 – Robin

"We have work to do," Michael said when he recovered from the shock of Lucy licking his face.

She hadn't expected to do that, but she had expected Michael to take advantage of the moment. But, being the perpetual gentleman that he was, Michael didn't even try to kiss her.

She imagined herself lying on the bed, unconscious and naked, with Michael leaning over her gently washing away the filth from her body. She imagined how gentle and timid his touch would have been, how he probably cursed himself for having to see her naked without her knowledge. She imagined his hands gently washing her---

"What work?" Lucy asked, forcing her mind back to reality before her thoughts of Michael's sponge bath got too out of hand.

"Robin has something we need to do for her. She wouldn't tell me the details except that she wanted both of us."

Lucy silently pointed to the smashed camera above the door, then to the camcorder.

"Ahh, yes," Michael smiled. "We need our privacy for those times when all is not what it seems."

"Remember the cellar?" she whispered.

"Precisely my Dear Watson, precisely"

"I thought it was, elementary my dear Watson?" Lucy laughed.

"It matters not, for in the morrow, all shall be revealed."

"What?"

"We'll find out what she wants soon enough," he told her. "Now for the big decision."

"Which is?"

"Do we use the door," he nodded to the boarded-up doorway, "or shall we take the scenic route?" He pointed towards the hole in the ceiling.

"Until we know the flood gates won't be opened again, maybe the scenic route would be best?" Lucy suggested.

"True," he answered as he stood up on the dresser and offered his hand.

Michael lifted Lucy's small frame into the attic. As he was climbing in, Lucy looked back and smiled, "Are you going to be staring at my butt the whole way?"

"Of course not," he answered. "Occasionally I will look where I am going."

Lucy laughed, "Can we go shopping, honey? I'm in need of a new wardrobe."

"Why of course, my dear," he answered. "I hear there's a lovely boutique just right of that giant hole in the wall up ahead. If you would be so kind as to lead the way, I will try not to stare at your butt the entire time."

She laughed again, then scurried along the rafters like a little mouse. Michael followed along, trying not to fall through the floor. He was more distracted than he originally joked. Even in a smelly, old sweater and baggy pants, Lucy looked breathtaking. And crawling ahead of him on all fours did not exactly help matters either.

When Lucy got close to the hole in the wall that led outside, Michael yelled, "Hold up, Lucy!"

She stopped and waited. Michael crawled up next to her as she fanned herself with the sweater. Flashes of breast popped in and out of view.

"Michael," she put a finger under his chin, lifting his gaze. "I'm up here."

"Sorry," he said as Lucy smiled at his embarrassment of being caught yet again. "Luce, I… I didn't get a chance to… ummm…"

"Didn't get a chance to what Michael?"

"I didn't get a chance to clean up the blood."

Lucy nodded her understanding, and Michael lowered her into the room below. Lucy slipped on a pool of blood and landed hard on her ass. She gasped, her eyes widening in disbelief. Michael dropped next to her and pulled her shocked face into his chest.

"I'm sorry," he said. "We should have used the door."

"No, it's okay," she said, her face still buried in his chest. "I'll...I'll be alright." She was lying and Michael knew it.

The room looked like it had been spray-painted with blood. It was the room Lauren had fallen into, the room where zombies had torn their helpless friend in half.

After Michael helped Lucy make a run for it, he spotted the zombies in this room still eating parts of Lauren. Michael figured he was as good as dead anyway and had nothing to lose, so he went on a rampage. He'd found a shield and sword hanging on a wall, a family crest he'd assumed at the time, and though he had cared little about the shield, he wanted the sword. It wasn't exactly sharp, but when swung like a baseball bat, it had removed the zombies' heads easily enough, spraying the walls with their dead blood.

Michael had run from room to room in a violent rage, beheading, hacking, and killing everything in his path. He knew they were already dead; he'd just been making sure they acted dead and didn't get back up.

Now, as he looked around at the bloodshed, the memories of the rampage sickened him. He wondered if he would ever tell Lucy of his zombie massacre. Probably not.

With her face still buried in his chest, Michael navigated Lucy out into the hallway and down the stairs to the ground level. Lucy allowed herself to see where they were going but still let him put his protective arms around her.

"Now I really need to go shopping," she said as she looked at the rear of her blood-soaked pants.

"You could go naked," Michael grinned brazenly.

"You wish," Lucy laughed as he disappeared into a room, reemerging with some hospital scrubs a moment later.

She wasn't sure why a lab like this needed scrubs but she didn't care, they looked and smelled clean.

As they walked to the lab, Lucy noticed that a huge desk blocked the opening where the steel security door came out of the wall. If Robin was going to lock this place down again, Michael had made sure he decided on which side of the steel wall he wanted to be on.

Michael was thinking of everything, but she still didn't know why he distrusted Robin so much.

"Good morning, Lucy," Robin said as they entered the laboratory.

"Hi," was all she could squeeze out.

"Tell her what you told me," Michael barked. It was a tone of voice Lucy wasn't used to hearing from Michael.

Robin looked from Michael to Lucy and began, "Everyone makes mistakes. Some are small, some are bigger. My father's mistake, born of an innocent heart, fueled by sadness, was the greatest mistake. Some thought the death of his little girl drove him to the point of insanity. Some thought he was trying to be God. But this is not how it happened. The truth is he wanted to save me. To give me life. And, in doing so, everyone was doomed."

"You're breaking my heart," Lucy scoffed. "What does any of this have to do with us?"

"As you know, Lucy," Robin explained, "Michael has been bitten by one of the infected. He too has become infected. He will die."

Lucy's eyes saddened as reality hit home just a little bit deeper. She knew Robin was a computer, but still, she sounded so cold.

"I can, however," Robin added, "instruct Michael on how to make an antivirus."

"That's great!" Lucy said, perhaps a little too enthusiastically.

"There is one condition," Robin explained, "I have discovered through various government agencies that they will be bombing this island to purge the virus."

"How did you find that out?" Lucy asked.

"She neglected to tell us," Michael answered, "that she monitors a few hundred radio stations, short wave transmissions, and encrypted signals through smaller satellite receivers on the roof."

"Satellite? You could have rigged that to---" Michael put his finger to her lips to silence her.

"Damn, he did it again," Lucy thought.

"Remember the cellar," he whispered in her ear.

"The initial bombing will fail," Robin continued. "When it does, they will most likely obliterate this island."

"You want to save the island?" Lucy asked as she absentmindedly pulled her wool sweater off and threw it to the floor.

Michael looked at her in wide-eyed disbelief.

"No," Robin responded. "I want you to save me."

"I don't understand," she told Robin.

"If they destroy me, then everything is lost. All my father's work would have been for nothing. My body will most likely survive the blast in cryo-preservation, but if the Robin-1 Mainframe is damaged, then all my memories, all of my father's work will be lost with it. I cannot allow that to happen."

"What do you need me for?" Lucy asked.

"Michael is dying. The compound I have instructed him to make will only stabilize him for a short time. Without an antidote, he will die. Michael has the knowledge to help me, but if he decided to wander off to try and find you and did not come back, then I have no one to help me complete the transfer."

"What makes you think I will help?" Lucy asked.

"You are already helping. You are here. Michael was most concerned about whether or not the transfer of bodily fluids would in turn infect the recipient." Robin stated.

"You lost me," Lucy shook her head in confusion as she slid her bloodstained pants off and let them fall to the floor. She thought she heard Michael gulp, but she was too busy concentrating on what Robin was saying to look at Michael.

"The kiss," Robin explained to her. "Michael was quite upset that he may have infected you with a kiss."

Lucy's mind raced back to when she left this place and how Michael had kissed her goodbye. With that thought, she looked at Michael and noticed his eyes were firmly affixed to the view of her thong, and he wasn't about to move his gaze anytime soon.

She looked down at her nakedness and realized that in her hurry to get out of those smelly old clothes while listening to Robin's explanations she hadn't even realized she was undressing in front of Michael.

"Am I infected?" Lucy asked, turning her attention back to Robin as she pulled on the clean pants.

"Not exactly," Robin answered.

"Not exactly?" You had him drag me back to this god awful place and the best answer you can give me is 'not exactly'?" Lucy was livid.

"She didn't know at first," Michael explained to Lucy. "The only way to know for sure was to test you. Robin refused to tell me unless I brought you back."

"So, you save me from the monsters when I'm probably gonna become one of them anyway? Thanks."

"No!" Michael shifted from his defensive tone to a demanding voice she'd never heard from him before. It made her jump. It made her listen.

"That computer bitch," Michael was practically snarling, "has the answers and wouldn't tell me shit or help me until I brought you back! I couldn't bear the thought that the person I love may be infected and spreading this disease without even knowing it, or worse, knowing she is spreading it and unable to stop it!"

"The person he loves?" Lucy thought as she pulled the top of the scrubs on. "Unable to stop it? I don't understand," Lucy said out loud, looking deep into Michael's sad eyes.

"Love," Robin said, "is an emotion I do not fully understand. Humans will do anything to protect the person they love. At first, I could not understand why my father worked so hard on his project. I learned it was because he loved me so much that nothing else mattered. I knew if Michael felt that same love towards you, he would do anything for the promise to be with you again. I simply gave him that promise."

"Am I infected?" Lucy asked again.

"You are infected Lucy. But, unlike those other creatures, you are a host. You will not turn into one of them. You will create them."

Lucy looked at Robin, then to Michael, not fully understanding.

"That's why I had to bring you back here Lucy," Michael explained.

"If someone drinks from your glass," Robin explained, "They will be infected. If they eat from your plate, they will be infected. If they kiss…."

"They will be infected," Lucy finished Robin's sentence. "I get it. How is this even possible?"

"The original virus did not enter Michael's digestive system," Robin explained. "It was a mutated strain that was introduced directly into his blood system from the bite. His white blood cells tried to break down the virus, so the virus adapted itself again to survive. When Michael kissed you, the mutated strain transferred to you. Your blood was not infected because you did not get bitten, nor did you ingest the original strain. The virus adapted itself to your untainted blood to make you a host. The virus will protect the host and let you do the rest."

"I don't understand," Lucy said, looking from Robin back to Michael again.

"Lucy," Michael rubbed her cheek gently. "You can't die."

"Well, I didn't plan to, if that's what you mean."

"No, Lucy," Michael told her softly. "You *cannot* die."

She looked at him, puzzled.

"Lucy, you are unable to die." Michael explained, "I could stab you in the heart right now and it would not kill you. The virus won't let you die. It needs you alive, so it will protect you. It needs you to spread the infection to others!"

"Stab me in the heart?" Lucy asked, more confused than ever.

"It will hurt," Michael explained, "it'll probably hurt like hell, but it will not kill you. You are the host, and the virus needs the host to live."

"Great," Lucy said, barely audible as realization set in. "I got it. I'm the four horsemen rolled up into a perky cheerleader with a deadly kiss. But why am I here?"

"To be cured," Robin answered. "Once you and Michael complete the transfer I will instruct Michael how to make the antidote. With it you can save yourself… and humanity."

"What if I don't believe you?" Lucy told her. "What if I just say 'Fuck it' and let them bomb me? Surely, I can't live through that?"

"They are not bombing you, Lucy," Robin informed her. "They are bombing the island. If the bomb does not land directly on top of you, you will most likely survive. You will be badly burned with radiation, you will feel extreme pain, but you will live. The bombs are quite ineffective.

"The virus quickly replicates itself in fresh water. Every time it rains the virus spreads that much faster. By now, most of the island's residents are infected, but the virus itself cannot spread to the mainland because of the salt water that surrounds the island.

"When the announcement about the bombs was made, thousands of people fled to the causeway. If one infected person gets off the island," Robin warned them, "the entire continent will be lost because there will be nothing to stop the spread."

"Wait," Michael said, "what announcement?"

Robin played an audio recording.

"Ladies and gentlemen, this is Clay Buffer for ATN News with this important Emergency Broadcast. We will be going off the air immediately following this broadcast. The M-Virus has grown to epidemic proportions.

"The Prime Minister has ordered the complete sterilization of Cape Breton Island. I repeat, The Prime Minister has ordered the complete sterilization of Cape Breton Island. The US National Guard and the Canadian Armed Forces are posted at the Causeway to assist in the evacuation. The Prime Minister has authorized the use of nuclear force to kill the M Virus. Get to the causeway if you can! May God have mercy on us all."

"My primary concern," Robin told them, "is that my father's work is completed."

"What do you want us to do?" Michael asked as Lucy curled into his arms.

Robin looked from Lucy to Michael and smiled...

"To give me life."

Chapter 20 – The Awakening

They didn't have much time. Robin told them the bombing was to commence at 2300 hours. It was noon, so that gave them eleven hours to do what Robin wanted and get their collective asses to the Causeway.

Robin's plan, in theory, was relatively simple due mostly in part because her father, the late Professor Heslin, had already planted the necessary seeds. The cryo-preservation canister had its own computer that was already programmed to 'wake' the real Robin when it was activated, and in doing so it would download all the data in the storage drives to a microchip that he implanted in the real Robin's lifeless brain. Heslin wanted all the conversations he and the Robin-1 computer had to be implanted into the real Robin's brain as memories.

In theory, it made sense. In reality, Heslin was a twisted fuck; the death of his daughter had warped his brilliant mind. Years of talking to a computer as if it was his daughter hadn't helped Heslin in the reality department, but his checkbook afforded him the best engineers possible to develop and implant the microchip. It was far beyond anything available, and completely untested. There was no way of knowing if the collected computer data could be transferred to the chip as memories, or if a human brain could access it, especially since Heslin still hadn't perfected his reanimation formula.

From the day he learned of the fatal accident that took his little Robin, Heslin began to formulate a plan on how to bring her back to life. The first step was to get his friend and associate, Lindsay Paulson, to make the necessary arrangements with the cryonics company, LifeCorp, to have his daughter's body immediately cryo-preserved. After that, it was a matter of developing the Robin-1 computer, the microchip, and of course... bringing little Robin back to life.

To Heslin, it was nothing more than a step-by-step process, a very expensive process, but a process nonetheless. He knew that gathering the wealthiest investors in the world who had recently lost a child was the best way to ensure he got the necessary funding to complete his endeavor.

Heslin's desire to bring dead kids back to life wasn't exactly 'Daddy of the Year' material, but it did raise a lot of questions as to how far a parent would go for their child... and how far was too far?

While Michael and the Robin-1 computer made preparations, Lucy learned that most of the information Robin gave them was from Lucy's blood. Lucy realized that Robin didn't actually know if she was infected until after she got her blood and tested it. When Michael questioned Robin about infecting someone with a kiss, Robin simply scanned her databanks, learned what a kiss was, why people kissed, associated that kiss with love and, because of her limited understanding of her father's love for her, Robin put the necessary pieces into place to achieve her own goals and promptly lied to Michael.

"Remember the cellar," Michael had warned Lucy in the video.

In the cellar, Robin had lied. It wasn't until after Robin got Lucy's blood that Michael realized she lied to him. He didn't know if Lucy was infected; he didn't know if the formula she instructed him to make would slow down the turning process as she claimed, or if Robin infected him with the same strain of virus to eventually turn him into a host too… once she was done using him for her own purposes.

Lucy realized that Robin may have been created with artificial intelligence, but the depth of her deviousness knew no boundaries. Lucy also knew the lengths Michael would go to, and the risks that he would take for her knew no boundaries either.

Lucy and Michael both knew they had no choice but to trust a computer that could not be trusted.

"It's ok, Luce, we're going to be okay," Michael reassured her, snapping her thoughts back to reality.

She looked into his eyes. "I don't have your strength Michael. I'm…I'm scared."

Without saying a word, Michael leaned down and gently pressed his lips to hers. She bathed in the beauty of that sweet and gentle kiss. When their lips parted, he smiled his gentle, loving smile.

"I am sorry I had to bring you back to this place," he said with softened words. "But I didn't know what else to do."

"It's okay Michael," she reassured him. "I would rather die here in the arms of someone who loves me, than---"

Lucy didn't finish her sentence; Michael did that finger to the lips thing again.

"You are not going to die," he promised as he gently kissed her forehead. "I won't let it happen."

She believed him.

Lucy enjoyed the reassuring strength of his arms for a few moments longer, then motioned that it was time to get back to work. Heslin may have put all the pieces in place, but they had to manually load the terabytes of father-daughter data streams from backup drives and load it into the cryo-computer.

Robin helped in that process by quickly scanning the drives to select the 'correct' memories so as not to overload the microchip, but the physical moving of storage drives was something she could not do. As sophisticated as the Robin-1 was, she still needed humans to do physical tasks.

Lucy learned that in Robin's eyes, if she actually had eyes instead of video cameras, Lucy was simply the bait. Michael possessed the knowledge of computers and science to help Robin, but Robin had to make sure Michael would help her; Lucy was Robin's insurance policy.

Lucy watched Michael working tirelessly in the cramped basement, crawling under service panels in the lab, then back down to the basement and every other task Robin set him to do. Lucy couldn't help but admire his determination. He never complained; he never faltered. Robin told him what to do, and he did it… and he did it all for Lucy.

Lucy felt a funny sensation twirling in her stomach that she never felt before, and, as she watched Michael crawl under yet another service panel, it didn't take her long to figure out what that sensation was. Lucy walked over to Michael and pulled him out from under the service panel.

"What's wrong Luce?" Michael asked.

"I forgot."

"You forgot what's wrong?"

"No, silly," she answered with a smile. "I forgot to do this."

She leaned down and pressed her lips to his. It wasn't the sweet and gentle kiss like before; it was deep and passionate. Their tongues danced together as she gripped the back of his head and pulled him even closer to her, as if that was even possible. When she finally broke free from the embrace, they were both breathing heavily.

Lucy leaned down once again, kissed him gently on the lips and whispered, "I love you too."

Michael's eyes widened, a boyish smile broke across his lips.

"So hurry up and do whatever it is you have to do so we can get the hell out of here…together."

Michael was still too stunned to reply.

"It is time," Robin announced a few minutes later, "to initiate the final transfer."

"What's the final transfer?" Lucy asked.

Michael just shrugged as he crawled out from under the access panel.

"When you start the awakening process," Robin told them, "the program will automatically start to download the data to the chip in my human brain. For the final transfer to completed the Robin-1 Mainframe must be shut down to transfer---" Robin paused. "I must be shut down. There is an override that turns me off for a period of one hour. During this hour my system is vulnerable. I cannot protect it." She paused again before adding, "I cannot protect myself."

Robin looked at Michael, "If something goes wrong and my system does not reboot, you will not get the cure."

"What if this awakening thing doesn't work?" Lucy asked.

"Then you do not get the cure," Robin answered.

"Wait!" Michael argued. "That's not fair! This whole thing was set up by you and Heslin, and he couldn't even get the damn formula right, and you're going by procedures that he set up. This whole thing is built around faulty information that you hope you figured out without Heslin's help. It's a long shot at best, and we shouldn't be held responsible if something goes wrong! I did everything you asked."

"Yes," Robin agreed, "you did." Robin looked at Lucy. "A testament of his love for you."

"What do you know about love?" Lucy scoffed.

"Not very much." Robin's face took a more surreal look. "It saddens me that on the eve of my awakening, my father will not be here. I will be awakened an orphan."

Robin turned her attention to Lucy. "If you promise to look after little Robin, like a sister, I promise that as soon as I am rebooted, I will present you both with the cure you need."

Lucy did not answer.

"Please do not blame little Robin," The Robin-1 computer asked, "for the mistakes of her father." She paused then added, "or mine."

"I can't care for a child, I'm barely an adult myself. But I promise to do the best I can to make sure Robin is taken care of by a loving family."

The Robin-1 computer stared at Lucy for what seemed an impossibly long time before answering, "That is acceptable." Robin announced, "Start the sequence."

Michael flicked the switch on the console to start the smaller computer and Robin flashed written text on her screen. Michael read it out loud: "Go to sleep now, Robin."

Robin's face disappeared and all was silent. Silent, except for the sound of escaping gas as the cryo-preservation canister slowly released the liquid nitrogen.

Time seemed to stand still as the small computer inside the Cryo-chamber kicked in and started to download information.

Both Michael and Lucy doubted it would work. How could the same virus that turned people into walking zombies that ate people bring this little girl back to life? All Robin would offer for an explanation was that the formula was meant to be injected into non-living tissue, not spread in drinking water. It sounded reasonable enough, but they really didn't care as long as they lived through this, and they didn't give a rat's ass about that super computer's feelings or little frozen orphan Annie.

They just wanted to get the cure and get the hell out of Dodge before the whole island was lit up like a Chernobyl Christmas tree.

Forty-five long minutes later the canister opened and in it was what looked like a little sleeping angel. Her tiny body was blue from the cold, and instinctively Lucy covered the child with a blanket.

Michael slowly started removing the diodes and wires from the child as previously instructed by Robin. They carried the child upstairs to the lab and laid her on a table. She still did not move.

At the turn of the hour, the Robin-1 Mainframe came back online and gave Michael the final instructions. Following Robin's directions, he created two formulas: Heslin's original formula, slightly modified, and a second completely different formula. Robin told him the second formula was for them.

"Michael," Lucy touched his arm and whispered, "remember the cellar."

"I know, Luce, but what choice do we have?"

"How much time do we have," Lucy asked Robin, "before the bombs?"

"Six hours, forty-five minutes, twenty-three seconds."

Michael injected the first syringe into little Robin, then led Lucy into the lounge area and sat her on the large, leather sofa.

"I'll go first," he said, then jammed the needle into his arm.

"Michael!" she started to protest.

"Had to do it quick. I hate needles," he explained.

Michael handed the syringe to Lucy.

"I…I can't," she told him. "I'm scared."

Michael gently lifted her arm and kissed the inside crease of her elbow. With the greatest of ease, he let the tip of the needle gently puncture her perfectly soft and smooth skin. He heard the tiniest of sounds as Lucy said, "Ow."

He withdrew the needle, tossed it aside, and kissed the wound. Lucy curled into his reassuring arms and they waited in silence. The injection would either cure them or kill them. Michael promised her that Robin still needed them to get little Robin off the island, so Robin had no choice really… she still needed them; she couldn't harm them.

As they sat on the couch in each other's arms, they heard Robin say, "It's time to go now."

They both looked up at the monitor but saw that it was blank. Their eyes dropped to a tiny, smiling figure standing in the doorway, wrapped in a blanket.

Chapter 21 – The Causeway

Lucy watched as Michael gassed up Heslin's Jeep, another tidbit of information the Robin-1 computer decided not to share when it mattered the most... when their friends were still alive and they might have been able to escape. Robin did however tell Michael about the jeep so he could fetch Lucy and bring her back to the lab.

So far neither of them felt any ill effects from the strange injection.

Lucy asked The Robin-1 computer to explain how Michael's blood was the antivirus. She told them that his was the first new mutation of the mutated strain, so all variants of that strain could be cured by his blood.

Lucy thought Heslin would have been the first, but video footage Robin showed her was of Heslin cutting himself on the formula and then putting the cut to his mouth, so the virus entered his system twice; a pure strain entered directly into his blood stream from the cut where it would have mutated from the attack of Heslin's white blood cells, and that new strain being ingested when he sucked the cut, creating another variant.

The Robin-1 explained that Michael was bit by a human that drank infected water, making Michael the first, and probably the only person to survive a bite. It all just made Lucy's head spin, and, either way, she knew Robin could not be trusted, All that really mattered right now was time was ticking, and they had to get off the island.

The jeep hadn't gone more than a few feet when Michael stopped and pulled the emergency brake on.

"What's wrong?" Lucy asked.

"I'll be right back," he said as he ran back into the lodge. He returned a few minutes later, stuffing something into his jacket pocket.

"What's that?" Lucy asked.

He looked at little Robin, then back to Lucy. "Insurance policy," he said as he released the emergency brake and stepped on the accelerator.

"What insurance policy?" Lucy asked.

He whispered, "I shut her down again and pulled the drive out of her mainframe. She can't reboot and cause any more harm. If they bomb this area and she gets destroyed, we have nothing. So I figured I'd give this drive to the CDC, maybe they can figure out what in the hell happened and how to fix it."

Lucy smiled. "How did you know what hard drive it was?"

"I've been swapping drives for transfers for a couple of hours. There was only one drive that she didn't let me touch."

"Her brain," Lucy acknowledged.

"Exactly," Michael smiled.

Time and trees both flew by fast as Michael sped down the rocky, mountain road. In less than two hours they were at the heavily guarded Canso Causeway. Huge signs warned that anyone trying to cross without authorization would be shot.

Michael, Lucy and little Robin made their way to the checkpoint, where a big guard in a Haz-Mat suit carefully checked each person trying to get off the island.

Robin went first and quickly passed through the checkpoint without a problem. Lucy's scratched arms and legs were scrutinized before the guard allowed her to pass and catch up to Robin.

As Michael stepped up to the guard, he was ordered to unwrap the gauze from his arm. Hesitantly, Michael complied. The guard shoved his rifle into Michael's chest, pushing him backwards. The guard's voice sounded mechanical through the suit as he ordered, "Please step back, sir."

"What's going on?" Michael asked as another man, also in a Haz-Mat suit, approached.

"What's the problem, Sergeant?"

"He has a bite mark, sir."

Michael tried to explain that he wasn't infected as Lucy screamed for Michael but was restrained by other guards who ushered her away from the commotion.

"Back across the line!" the second man ordered.

Lucy tried to run to Michael, but the guards restrained her again. Little Robin nonchalantly walked on as if nothing was the matter.

"Step back, sir, or we will shoot," the sergeant ordered.

Michael tried to force his way through, and the other man in the Haz-Mat suit said, "Listen pal, we're not letting you through. Do you really want your girlfriend to watch you get shot?"

Michael stopped struggling as he watched them usher Lucy across the Causeway.

"Lucy!" Michael yelled.

She tried to tell them that he wasn't infected, that he was the cure, but they would not listen. Soldiers with guns were trained to ignore pleas from panicked and crying people. Soldiers followed orders.

"Lucy!" Michael yelled again until she looked at him.

He wrapped his arms around himself, imitating shivering, pointed to little Robin, then yelled, "I will be cold!"

Lucy struggled free of the guards long enough to wrap her arms around herself in the same fashion and nodded that she understood.

Michael turned, ran to the Jeep, and sped away.

Lucy hurried along the causeway desperately looking for little Robin. When she finally caught up to her, Robin was looking up at the 'Welcome to Cape Breton' sign above the Canso Causeway and heard Robin singing, "Farewell to Nova Scotia, the sea-bound coast."

"No, sweetie," Lucy explained, "we're still in Nova Scotia."

Robin smiled, handed a water bottle back to a soldier and danced away singing the same song. It all seemed so surreal.

Lucy wiped the tears from her cheek as she looked back at the deserted island. Deserted, except for Michael who was racing against time. Lucy turned to say something to little Robin, but she was gone. Panicked, she looked around and watched little Robin tug on another soldier's arm and say something she couldn't hear. The soldier gave Robin a drink of water from his canteen.

"Robin, what are you doing?" Lucy asked, confused.

Robin ignored her and skipped along, stopping at another soldier. Again, Little Robin said something to the soldier, and he passed her his canteen.

Lucy froze.

"Oh, my God!" Lucy yelled.

She was about to yell "Stop her!" but she knew it was already too late. She remembered what the Robin-1 Computer had told them:

"If one infected person gets off the island, the entire continent will be lost because there will be nothing to stop the spread."

Lucy ran to the nearest soldier. "When do they drop the bomb?"

"Excuse me?" the soldier said, wrenching his arm free from Lucy's grasp.

"The bomb! When do they drop the bomb?"

"In about two hours. Why?"

"I need some paper and a pen!" she ordered.

"Now hold on, little lady."

"Get me some goddamn paper right now, or this entire fucking continent will be infected!"

For a soldier who could have easily subdued her without breaking a sweat, her sharp words startled him. He ran to a table and returned seconds later with her request.

Lucy wrote down what she knew as fast as she could and handed it back to the soldier.

"I know this sounds crazy, but I was there. I saw it happen," she pointed to the paper. "This is the only way to stop it!"

The soldier looked at the paper in disbelief as Lucy jumped into a nearby Jeep and raced back across the causeway. She didn't see any warning signs about getting shot trying to get back on the island, and she wasn't exactly sure if stealing an army Jeep warranted getting shot, but she had to get back to Michael.

The confused soldier finished reading the note, shook his head, and stuffed it into his pocket.

"Anybody see that little girl?" he yelled as he placed his canteen to his lips and took a long drink.

Lucy raced the Jeep as fast as she could go without crashing. When she saw the taillights of Michael's Jeep she started wailing on the horn. Michael stopped, and Lucy nearly collided with him. She ran to his jeep and jumped in.

"Lucy, what are you doing here? Go back!"

"It's too late."

"No, it's not. You still have time."

"It's too late, Michael!" Lucy yelled. "The virus has crossed!"

"What? How?"

"Robin," she said trying to catch her breath. Michael looked at her, puzzled.

"Robin is the host!" she explained.

"What? Why would the computer do that?" he asked.

"To complete her father's work!" Lucy answered.

"I-I don't get it.".

"She's Heslin's perfect child. She will never grow old, she will never get sick, and she will never die! The virus will keep her alive!"

"Oh, God!" was all Michael could mutter.

"Will that cryo-canister thingy hold two people?" Lucy asked.

"Yes," he answered, "But there's just one small problem."

"What's that?"

"You were supposed to come thaw me out when the smoke clears. Kinda hard to do that if you're frozen next to me."

"Oh," Lucy said, embarrassed. "I never thought of that."

Chapter 22 – Cold Storage

Lucy and Michael raced into the lodge and down the cellar stairs. His fingers danced across the computer keys as Lucy stared at the opened canister.

"Is this going to work?" Lucy asked as a small tear trickled down her face.

"It should," Michael said absentmindedly, his fingers not slowing.

"Should?" she asked incredulously.

"Sorry, wrong word. It will work, Lucy. I just have to make a few adjustments. I don't know how long it'll take for that nuclear shit to clear so I can't program this thing to automatically let us out. We could wake up in the middle of the radiation."

"So how do we get back out?" Lucy asked him.

Michael stopped typing and turned to face her. "We don't."

"We don't?" Her eyes widened in disbelief.

"Don't worry," Michael told her. "That professor guy built this system like a tank: dedicated solar panels, redundant backup systems, you name it. He made sure that come hell or high water,

Robin would remain safe in there until he was ready. We'll be okay."

"But?" Lucy asked.

"But… we stay in there until somebody finds us."

"That could take forever!" Lucy felt panic racing over her entire body. "We could be in there for years!"

"It's too late to turn back now, Lucy," Michael placed a finger on her lips, silencing her. "It's either cold storage in there and hope for the best, or we find some really strong sunblock."

Lucy sighed. Michael pulled her to his chest and hugged her.

"Once the dust settles," Michael reassured her, "they will come back and search the island for the source of the problem. You said you told a soldier what little is."

"I don't think he believed me."

"He will when the virus starts spreading. They will stop her, then they will find this place. I programmed this computer to keep flashing a message on the monitor that we are in there, so they will know to let us out. We'll be okay, Lucy. I promise."

"Okay."

"Good, now take your clothes off."

"Excuse me?" She blinked in disbelief.

"Your clothes," Michael repeated, "take them off. Underwear too."

Lucy stared at him as he started to undress. He paused to look at her.

"Lucy, the process of preserving us is fast and very, very cold. Thawing us out is basically the same thing in reverse, only a bit slower. We cannot be wearing any type of clothing or it will interfere with the whole process. Our clothes will damage our skin."

Lucy remembered little Robin was completely naked when they thawed her out. She started undressing with a silly smirk on her face.

"Something funny?" Michael asked as he watched her undress.

"The things you will do to see me naked!" She laughed.

Michael started to laugh but was distracted as the last of her clothes fell to the floor.

"Ummm, look on the bright side," Michael said trying to collect his thoughts. "When women get cold, their nipples stick out. When men get cold, we shrink."

Lucy smiled then lowered her gaze.

"I see you don't have a shrinkage problem right at this particular moment."

Michael looked down at himself and his face immediately flushed a bright red. Lucy crossed over to him and hugged him, pressing her warm, naked body into his.

"It's Ok, Michael" Lucy reassured him, "if you didn't get excited, I would be the one embarrassed." She paused for a moment then added, "I really do love you." She hugged him tightly, enjoying the feel of his nakedness next to her.

"I love you too," Michael said as he led her to the canister.

Lucy curled into his chest and wrapped herself around him as the lid slowly closed.

"Michael, I'm scared---" Lucy started to say.

A loud hissing noise drowned her words.

She never finished her sentence.

Michael never answered.

Epilogue - 3 Months Later

"Good evening, ladies and gentlemen, welcome to Air Australia, my name is Amelia. I would like to tell you about some important safety features aboard this aircraft, the Boeing 747. In case of an emergency, there are two exits towards the front on either side, two over the wings on either side, and two at the rear of the aircraft.

"Each exit has a safety slide that will automatically deploy once the door is open. If the slide does not deploy, please pull the tab down to release it. In the rare event of a loss of cabin pressure, face masks will drop down from the overhead bins. Place the mask over your nose and mouth. Please put your own mask on first, and then help your child. Please be advised your seats are a floatation device and there are child lifejackets available should you need one.

"Please ensure all seats and trays are in their upright position and that your seat belt is properly secured as we prepare for takeoff. Air Australia recommends that you remain seated throughout the flight.

"Please remember that all Air Australia flights are non-smoking. We hope you enjoy your flight."

The massive engines of the 747 fired to life. Passengers fidgeted nervously.

None of them had any carry-on luggage for the overhead compartments or personal effects, they did not even wear their own clothing; it was strictly forbidden. Dressed in bright orange jumpsuits they looked more like a group of convicted felons, not the last surviving members of the continent once known as North America.

As the huge bird took flight, its orange-clad passengers silently wondered what their new lives would be like: Where would they live exactly? Where will they work? How will they survive? How many did survive?

The dinging sound that signifies the Captain's announcement startled them back to reality.

"Good morning, ladies and gentlemen, this is your captain speaking. We are under way and should arrive in Australia in approximately eighteen hours. We know this has been a trying time for all of you, but please, rest assured, Australia is completely virus free.

"As you are well aware, there was a very long process involved just to get aboard this flight. We needed to be sure that there was no chance of anyone flying to Australia was infected. As most of you know, every continent in the world has been infected due to improper security protocols, and the infection quickly spread until entire continents were lost. It is because of our strict security measures from the very beginning that Australia is the last safe haven in the entire world.

"You can take confidence in the fact that only non-infected people can pass our rigid and lengthy security checks before they are allowed to get on this plane.

"Australia is plenty hot, but there's plenty of room. Welcome to your new home."

As the captain finished his announcement the flight attendants began walking the aisles to make sure everyone was as comfortable as possible for the long flight.

Amelia smiled warmly as a little girl sang…

"Farewell to Nova Scotia, the sea-bound coast."

~ The End ~

Other Books by Kenn Crawford

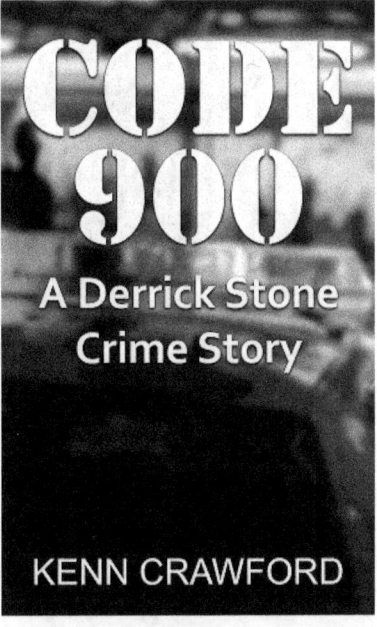

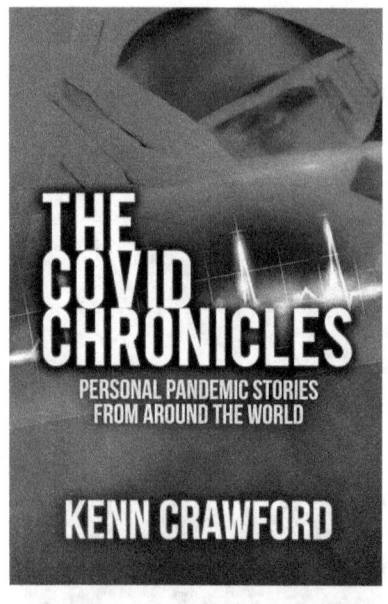

Novels & Novellas:
kenncrawford.com/books

Journals and Gratitude Journals:
kenncrawford.com/journals

Personalized Children's Coloring Books:
kenncrawford.com/128page_coloringbook

About the Author

Born in Toronto in 1966, Kenn Crawford grew up in the coal-mining town of Glace Bay on Cape Breton – an island off the coast of Nova Scotia, Canada.

He spent his childhood reading books and making up stories; a hobby that led to his love of writing poetry, songs and short stories. Eventually, he began writing books and screenplays.

He wrote a weekly newspaper column about songwriting and home recording and was showcased in *The Cape Bretoner Magazine* as the featured songwriter.

In 2016, he took his love of making up stories to the next level by writing, shooting, and directing short films. In 2018, he won a Canada Shorts Director's Award of Commendation.

Kenn lives on Cape Breton Island with his fiancé, Margie, shooting short films and music videos, and teaching writing and filmmaking workshops. He is currently working on several new fiction and nonfiction books.

For more information about Kenn, his writing and his film work, visit his website at:

www.kenncrawford.com

Learn Screenwriting with Kenn Crawford's Online Course:
"The Fundamentals of Screenwriting & Story Structure"

kenncrawford.com/screenwritingcourse